M/M Paranormal Romance

Javier Coven Book 2

Jayda Marx

Author's Note

Thank you for your interest in my book! This low angst, insta-love paranormal romance features my take on some seriously sexy vampires. They share many attributes of vampires found in other fictional works, but not all. This book contains dark elements, fated mates, moments so sweet they'll make your teeth tingle, and lots of laughs. I want my readers to finish my books with a smile on their face and a fierce case of the warm and fuzzies. Laughter is guaranteed, and each read delivers its own type of drama. Thanks again for taking a look and happy reading!

Prologue

Milo

I ducked my head as I entered the house, trying to make myself as inconspicuous as possible; it was the best way to survive here. Especially since I did something stupid tonight; so incredibly stupid.

"Where's my money?" Jerome barked before I could turn the corner to the hall that led to my bedroom; that is, if you consider a closet with a dirty cot shoved inside a bedroom. I pulled the wad of cash (a respectable $120) from my pocket and placed it on a small table without turning around. Jerome snatched it up and rifled through it. "Where's the rest of it?"

"It was a slow night," I replied quietly. Jerome growled and gripped my shoulder, spinning me around forcefully to face him.

"I always know when you're lying, you piece of shit." He shoved my chest and I winced at the flash of pain. His eyes narrowed. "What are you hiding?"

"Nothing," I lied again.

Jerome snarled as he gripped the collar of my t-shirt (one of three tops I owned) and tore it right down the middle, revealing a large bandage over the right side of my chest. "What the fuck is that?"

I knew there was no point in lying anymore. "It's a tattoo," I answered in a trembling voice.

He slapped me across the face and it took a moment for my eyes to refocus. "You spent my money on a fucking *tattoo*?" he growled through gritted teeth, spraying me with spit.

"It didn't cost anything," I replied quickly. Actually, I was trying out a new corner next to a tattoo parlor. I'd only made forty bucks by the time the owner of the shop came out. I thought he'd shoo me away, but instead he offered me a deal. Long story short, I took him around the world in exchange for the wing tattoo that now spread across my collar bone. I knew it was stupid, and I knew I'd pay for it later by Jerome's hand, but at the time, I didn't care. I longed for something of my own; something Jerome couldn't take away. Something that made me smile and made me like even just a patch of the skin I was in. It was the only bright spot I had, and even as I now saw the rage burning in Jerome's eyes, I didn't regret it.

"You have one job," he spat at me again. "You know what happens when you fail to do that job."

How could I forget? I'd been under Jerome's rule for the past three years, ever since I ran away from the house I grew up in and my abusive piece of shit father when I was seventeen. I had no money and no plan and ended up on the streets. When Jerome and his friends found me, I thought I'd struck gold. They offered me a place to stay if I did a few odd jobs for them, and I jumped at the chance.

The "odd jobs" ended up being picking up drugs from Jerome's supplier and delivering them to him and his crew. I hated it; I'd never even gotten a detention in school and suddenly I was a criminal, but what choice did I have? The only solace I had was that I wasn't the person actually selling the product. But that didn't last long. Jerome soon added dealing to my job list, and I sucked at it. I wouldn't push or insist, and left my assigned spot if I saw kids; I wouldn't be the one to expose them to that shit. One of my only successful deals was to an undercover cop.

I was actually relieved, and took the officer back to the house we stayed in and used as a headquarters in the hopes he would raid the place, shut it down and release me from this hell, even if it meant I went to prison; it couldn't be worse than what I was dealing with. But just my luck, I sold to a dirty cop. When we reached Jerome, the two of them worked out a deal; me. The cop wanted a cut of the money from then on out in exchange for keeping his mouth shut and protection from the police force, but as a closure to the deal, he wanted a piece of the dumbass virgin kid that started this mess.

As it turned out, I gave a great blow job. The threat from Jerome saying he'd shoot me if I didn't was good motivation. At any rate, that act found me a new position in this shitty crew. Jerome's other men ran the drugs and I sold my body. If I refused, I got beat. If I didn't meet a certain cash quota a day, I got beat. I couldn't go to the cops, because of Jerome's guy on the inside. I tried to run away once, but Jerome's men found me and beat me until I was within an inch of my life. So I was stuck; forced to sell my body and give the cash to Jerome in exchange for a dirty cot in a closet.

Jerome's fist collided with the side of my face and I saw stars. "No food until it heals," he growled. That was always the second layer of my punishment. Not that it was much different than normal; I ate whatever scraps were left on Jerome's and his men's plates. I made the least amount of money for the crew, so I was at the bottom of the food chain, so to speak. They also found me disgusting because of my work, though they were the ones who forced me to do it.

Jerome ripped the bandage from my chest and shook his head at the sight of the black feathered wing. He took a knife from his pocket and popped out the blade to press it to the design on my skin. "I'd cut it off if the scar wouldn't hurt business," he snarled.

His lips curled up into an evil grin. "I've got a better idea." He dragged me into the kitchen and slammed me into a chair. Marcus and Andre, two other men who worked for Jerome, were seated at the table but didn't blink an eye at the way Jerome was manhandling me.

"Hold him down," he ordered the two men. Without question, they raised from their seats and pinned me to mine. It was unnecessary since I was so much smaller than them, but they seemed to draw delight from it. Jerome left the room and returned only a few moments later carrying his knife and an ink pen, which he snapped in half over a plate. "If you wanted a tattoo, you should have just asked."

He pressed my arm down on the table, dipped the tip of his knife in the ink, and carved into my wrist. As he cut, I gritted my teeth and kept my breathing slow and deep. It hurt so much worse than what the actual professional had done, but I didn't want to give Jerome the satisfaction of knowing I was in pain.

"There we go," he said when he was finished. He nodded for Andre and Marcus to admire his work and they all three burst out laughing. "Maybe this will help you remember your place. This is all you are and all you'll ever be." I looked down at my wrist, where the word 'whore' was engraved into my bloody skin. "Now get the fuck out of my sight."

The two men holding me down pushed me from my chair into the floor. I caught myself with my hands and hissed at the pain in my wrist, making all three men laugh again. I ran to my "room" and curled up on my cot. My arm throbbed, my face ached, my stomach growled and my soul was shattered. This was my life and I saw no way out.

Chapter One

Milo

"Oh god...oh shit...oh god..."

I rolled my eyes as the man above me chanted and cursed. I'd only been sucking him off for about two minutes and he already sounded ready to blow. Not that I cared; the faster this was over, the faster I could get paid and be on my way.

The asphalt of the alleyway was hard and wet under my knees and it was freezing out here. I was dressed in tight, threadbare jeans and a skimpy mint green cropped tank top which were no match for the cold November evening air, but it was all I had. My outfit was filthy too, but none of the assholes I serviced seemed to care. They just wanted me to fall to my knees or bend over for them.

"Yes!" The man screamed as he exploded into the condom that he didn't want to wear, but I insisted he did. The only thing I could be grateful to Jerome for was that he always sent me out for the evening with a pocket full of condoms. Not that he gave a shit about me, but if I caught something and died, I couldn't make him money. Plus, if word got out I was infecting everyone, business would dry up.

I grimaced at the heat of the man's release against my tongue, but was thankful I didn't have to taste it; not that I particularly enjoyed the flavor of latex, either. I dropped his dick from my mouth and stood up to face him, giving him a flirty smile.

"Okay, honey, that'll be twenty." I called all my clients honey; I didn't want to know their actual names, and it'd be bad business to call them assholes like I wanted to.

The man pulled off the condom and tossed it into a nearby dumpster. A smelly alleyway wasn't my ideal office choice, but I didn't like getting into vehicles with random men. He zipped up and gave me a shrug. "Nah, I don't think so."

"But that was the deal," I replied sternly. "We discussed price before we started. And you certainly seemed to enjoy yourself."

"But what are you gonna do about it if I don't pay?" he smirked. The guy wasn't that much taller than my five foot six, but he was quite a bit thicker than my near skeletal frame. Though his girth looked to be more fat than muscle, he could still easily tear me apart. On the other hand, so could Jerome.

"We agreed on twenty and that's what you're going to pay," I insisted again in my meanest voice. The man didn't look intimidated in the slightest, but I couldn't blame him; it was surely like being threatened by a mouse.

He smirked and reached into his pocket. *Finally! I can get Jerome's money and maybe go warm up in the gas station for a few minutes before my next trick.* But no, I couldn't have been that lucky. What he pulled out was an ivory colored handle. He flicked his wrist and a blade popped out. *God dammit! What is it with everyone wanting to stab me lately?* "I'm not paying anything, and you're not going to be around to tell anyone."

Well, shit. As terrible as my life was, I really wasn't ready for it to end; especially in a wet, cold alleyway. The garbage man would probably find my mutilated body in the dumpster, and wasn't that a lovely thought.

Just then, a roar sounded from the entrance to the alley, reverberating off the brick walls on either side of us, drawing both of our attention to the man approaching. He was huge; my best guess would be around six foot six, and holy hell, he was thick. Unlike Hair-trigger Harry over here, this man was a solid wall of muscle. His long, curly black hair fell below his shoulders, blowing back as he stormed towards us. His furrowed cinnamon-colored eyes popped against his golden skin, and his trimmed goatee drew attention to the sharp jaw bones at its corners. He was simultaneously the hottest and most terrifying man I'd ever seen in my life. My feet wanted to bolt, but my dick wanted me to stay, which was weird; not much excited me sexually anymore. And my poor brain was just scared shitless, so I remained rooted to the spot. I didn't know what the man wanted, but I'd soon find out since I couldn't look away.

*****

Bastian

"I'm glad we were able to come to an agreement," I told the owners of *Page Turners,* the bookstore where Ben used to work. I'd been working with them for weeks to try and settle on a price for their business at Dante's request. He wanted to buy the shop for Ben as a gift. His mate loved to read, and Dante loved to spoil him and had more money than he knew what to do with, so buying an entire store was no trouble for him. He said it worked out nicely because we had several new members to our coven after the whole debacle with Hugo dissipated, so this would open up more jobs. Plus, he thought it was humorous that the couple who owned the store had basically fired Ben for being gay, but that he'd be giving it back to him as a gift from his husband.

"It was a pleasure doing business with you," Mr. Turner smiled as he stuck out his hand for me to shake.

"Likewise," I lied. All of my dealings with the Turners thus far had been over the phone, and this was our first meeting in person. They were truly terrible people. I knew how they'd treated Ben, whom I cared for like a member of my family, and how that in turn affected Dante, who was my Coven Master as well as my best friend. Not to mention, I'd witnessed first hand how they treated their employees unbecomingly while I was here discussing business.

Though the *new* employees would be coven members only once the property became Dante's, I knew he'd give the current workers a nice severance package. The man was honorable and fair, which was more than I could say for the Turners. The only person they were nice to was me, and that was only because I was offering them money. I wanted to tell them I was as gay as a picnic basket just for spite, but I didn't want to ruin Dante's deal.

I stepped outside the shop and pulled on my wool coat to fight against the coldness of the evening. I took a deep breath of the bracing air to try and settle my nerves. For days, I'd had an uneasy feeling that I couldn't shake. At first, I assumed it was anxiety over this meeting with the distasteful Turners, but now that it was over, I couldn't use it as an excuse.

I stepped towards my SUV but stopped before I reached the door. Something deep inside me said not to return home, but to circle the block on foot instead. Vampires have a keen sixth sense when it comes to danger, so I always follow my gut instincts. I wasn't sure what the danger was, but I wouldn't ignore the clear sign my body was giving me.

I placed my keys back in my suit pocket and walked down the sidewalk. Everything was still and quiet except for a car passing now and then, or a passerby tightening their jacket to fight off their chill before ducking into one of the shops that lined the road.

When I rounded the corner behind the bookstore, however, the air changed. Electricity charged around me, dancing up my hands and arms. The hair on the back of my neck stood up and my fangs elongated. Something big was about to happen; my body was preparing for battle. I listened closely, keeping my steps quiet as I came upon a long alleyway.

"We agreed on twenty and that's what you're going to pay," a small voice spouted angrily. At the sound, electric sparks shot down my arms again. My fangs tingled and blood rushed to my groin. A smile broke out over my face as I realized the voice belonged to my soulmate. My body wasn't readying to fight; it was preparing to claim.

I'd been waiting for over three hundred years to meet my beloved; the man

I would cherish, protect, honor and love for all of my days. The one who would complete me. The one who would mend my soul for all time, as it had been aching and crying out for its match for centuries. When Dante found Ben, I was overjoyed for my dearest friend, but also envious. I wondered if the day would ever come when I would meet my own mate, and now I was merely feet away from him.

    I stepped around the edge of the building and peered down the alley. My breath caught at the first sight of my beloved. He was small; maybe only a couple of inches taller than Ben, and thin to the point of emaciation. I could see his hip bones jutting out between the top of his jeans and the bottom of his short shirt. His clothes were dirty and not nearly warm enough for the weather. My mate's needs were not being taken care of, but that would end today.

Messy dark blond hair which was in need of a good wash fell around his ears. Though he was in need of some TLC (which I would most gratefully provide), he was the most beautiful creature I'd ever seen. No one else would ever catch my eye or capture my attention. From this moment forward, my world revolved around this precious little man.

I wasn't oblivious to what was happening in the scene before me; my mate was arguing with a man about money in a dank alley, where the scent of semen, latex and shame hung in the air. I hated these circumstances for my beloved, but held no judgement toward him for it. I only wanted to make his life better; to shower him in love and luxury.

My thoughts were interrupted by the sight of the other man in the alley pulling a knife from his pocket. "I'm not paying anything, and you're not going to be around to tell anyone."

A roar of fury and anguish ripped from my chest. I would not allow anything to happen to my mate. As I thundered down the alleyway toward the men, I was hit with my beloved's arousal and fear at the sight of me. Pride and guilt warred within me; I never wanted to frighten him, but I couldn't let the threat against him go unanswered.

I gripped the offending man by the throat and slammed him into the bricks of the side of the building. I held him several inches from the ground so that we were face to face.

"You dare pull a weapon on this man?" I murmured through gritted teeth.

"He was trying to rob me!" he answered the best he could through the force of my hand around his throat.

My mate gasped and I turned my head to make sure he was okay. "I didn't! I wasn't!" he insisted, shaking his head quickly. I was about to tell him I believed him and that everything would be okay, but the man in my grip saw an opportunity when my attention was away from him, and stabbed the blade of his knife into my abdomen. "Oh god!" my beloved cried, slapping both of his hands over his mouth.

I pulled the blade free of my stomach and felt my skin quickly knitting back together. The offending man's eyes were wide with terror when I merely folded the knife and stuck it into my pants pocket without loosening my grip on him.

"You're a damn liar. Now, take out your wallet," I demanded. The man did as I asked with shaking hands. "Give this man the money you owe him." He pulled a twenty out and handed it to my mate, who stuffed it into his front pocket, his worried eyes still trained on my stomach. I appreciated his concern for me, but hated that he was having to endure the stress of these events; especially over something as trivial as twenty dollars.

I leaned in so that my face was nearly touching the one of the man before me. "The only reason I've decided not to kill you where you stand is that I don't want this man to have to endure the sight." The smell of urine permeated the air as the man who was so brave with the knife in his hand minutes ago pissed himself. I curled my lip at the stench and lowered him to the ground, but didn't release my hand. "If you ever so much as look at this man again, I won't be so generous. Now, get out of my sight."

Once my hand unwrapped from around his throat, the man took off like a shot down the alley without so much as a glance back. My mate was immediately at my side.

"Are you okay?" he asked quickly, inspecting my abdomen again. There was an inch long slice in my suit jacket, but luckily my wound had repaired itself before I lost any blood. I didn't want my poor mate to be frightened of the sight.

"I'm fine. It was nothing," I assured him. Now that the acrid stench of the vile man was gone, I deeply breathed in my mate's naturally sweet scent of butterscotch. It was intoxicating.

"It wasn't nothing," he insisted. "You saved my life." His beautiful blue-gray eyes finally met mine. "Thank you."

"You're most welcome." I gave him my warmest smile and his answering shy grin caused my heart to race. I wanted to reach out and tuck his wild hair behind his ears; to run my fingers along the smoothness of his cheeks, but I didn't want to do anything he may find too forward. There was, however, one thing I couldn't live without. "May I ask your name?"

"Falcon," he replied quietly. The dishonesty and guilt surrounding him told me it was a fake name. Given his circumstances, I understood the need for one. I hoped my beloved trusted me enough to tell me his real name soon.

"It's my greatest pleasure to meet you, Falcon. My name is Bastian Santos." I held my hand out to him. After a moment of hesitation, he placed his small hand in mine to shake. Warmth trailed up my arm at the contact, though his fingers were freezing. "Forgive me; I don't know where my manners are." I shrugged off my coat and offered it to Falcon. Longing shone in his eyes as he looked at the warm cloak, but he shook his head no.

"No thank you. I've...I've got to get back to work." His eyes fell to the ground and his shoulders slumped in defeat.

"Falcon, you don't have to do this any longer."

He huffed a humorless laugh. "I wish that were true. But if I don't..." he trailed off and shook his head. "I need to get back to work. Thank you again, Bastian." The sound of my name on his lips made my breath hitch. He turned around and began to walk toward the main road.

"Wait!" I begged and took one large step to catch up with him. "How much money do you make in a night?" I was desperate to find something to keep him with me. Now that I'd found my mate, I couldn't let him walk away.

Falcon narrowed his eyes in confusion before answering quietly, "I have to make two hundred."

I pushed away the thoughts of how busy he'd have to be each night to make two hundred dollars at twenty dollars a client. Again, I would never hold such things against my beloved, but I instantly wanted to kill every man who had ever laid a finger on him. I pulled out my wallet and handed over all of the cash inside, which totalled four hundred thirty seven dollars. Falcon's eyes widened as relief washed over him. After he stuffed the money into his pocket, he looked at me again and disappointment took over him once more. He forced a flirty smile onto his face.

"And what can I do for *you*?" My heart shattered. In Falcon's world, nothing came without a price. There were no kind gestures or good will.

"First, I ask that you take this." I offered him my coat again. He acquiesced, shrugging on the heavy wool and pulling the lapels closed around him. My pride swelled at the sight of him in my clothing. The coat was much too large for his thin, short frame, but I was happy to provide him with warmth. "And if you don't mind, I'd like to take you out to dinner." I didn't want to appear too pushy, but I needed my mate with me. I needed to make sure he was fed and warm and safe.

Falcon blinked at me. "Dinner? That's it?"

"I will also buy you dessert if you wish."

He blinked again. "No, I meant..."

"I know what you meant, Cielito," I interrupted him. "But please understand, what I most desire is to make sure *you* are taken care of tonight. Will you allow me this?" Falcon's mouth opened and closed a few times, but no words came out. The gratitude, happiness and affection rolling off of him, however, spoke volumes. I was indebted to my empathic link to him due to our bond. Finally, he nodded and pulled my coat tighter around him. "Thank you, Falcon. My SUV is this way." I motioned toward the end of the alley, but my mate looked uneasy. "If you prefer, I will escort you on foot," I offered. I wasn't thinking at first that he may not be comfortable riding with me yet.

Falcon chewed on his lip. "It *is* pretty cold out tonight." He still didn't seem sure though, and an idea struck me.

"I promise your safety, Cielito. In fact…" I took the knife I'd taken from the man out of my pocket and held it out to my mate. "Take this. I want you to feel secure; not only with me, but in general. You deserve to feel safe."

Falcon's eyes were huge as he took the knife from my fingers. He nodded once more and we walked to the end of the alley. "You know, you're kind of blowing my mind tonight," he admitted once we stepped out onto the sidewalk.

"I'm sorry."

He gave me a lopsided smile and my heart skipped a beat. "I meant it in a good way."

I stopped walking and faced him. "I know. I'm sorry because my actions don't reflect what you experience every day." His mouth gaped open a few more times. "My car is just ahead," I said, nodding in the direction of my vehicle.

I helped Falcon into the SUV and took my seat behind the wheel. I couldn't help but stare at him. I couldn't believe how beautiful he was, or that he was actually sitting here with me. My mate, my love, my everything was here beside me, and my heart was overflowing.

He squirmed under my gaze. "So um...is this the part where you say you'd rather forget about dinner and I just take my pants off?"

My heart shattered once more. "No, Cielito. This is the part where I ask you to buckle up so that you're safe for our drive." He blinked before fastening his seatbelt. "And I must apologize for staring. I don't mean to be rude or make you uncomfortable; it's just that you are the most gorgeous man I've ever laid eyes on."

Falcon still said nothing, but his confusion and arousal filled the interior of my vehicle. I hated that my man did not see his beauty or worth, but pleased he was affected by my appearance and presence. Not that I was surprised; mates were perfectly paired by Fate, but humans were unaware of such things. Most humans were unknowing of the paranormal beings that walked among them every day, let alone their culture and customs. I could only hope that when I'd earned my mate's trust and could divulge my identity to him, he would be as accepting and open as Ben was with Dante.

One advantage I had over Dante when he was wooing his mate is that I fed just this morning on the bagged blood from the medical wing at our apartment complex. It had tasted sour and was difficult to get down, but I refused to allow my hopes to climb at what it could mean. Now that Falcon sat beside me, I understood clearly. I could only take sustenance from the blood of my beloved for the rest of time, and it was what my body craved. I was glad to have fed recently so that I could take my time with Falcon without worrying about growing weak or negative consequences. My precious man needed assurance and for me to build his confidence before he was ready to hear my declarations.

And good lord, did I have declarations to share with him. Not only about my identity, but the fact that I wanted to support and care for him forever. That I would love him with all of my heart and soul for all time, and protect him with everything I was. But those words were not for now. It could take humans weeks, months, even years to feel the things vampires understood within moments of meeting their fated mates. Luckily, Falcon would feel the pull of our bond even if he didn't understand it, which would help with his acceptance. Still, now wasn't the time. For now, I needed to focus on taking care of my beloved.

"Where would you like to eat?" I asked as I pulled the SUV out into traffic, which was building steadily. I peeked over to Falcon, who looked stunned that the choice was his. "I'll take you anywhere you wish," I added.

"Oh, um...is pizza okay?" he asked after a moment of thought.

"Of course," I smiled, and again we fell into silence. There was so much I wanted to know about my mate; just to speak with him, but I also didn't want to push. I thought perhaps waiting until we were in a public place amongst other people would be best to start asking him personal questions. I drove a few blocks until I found a pizza chain restaurant. Since it was not one of our coven-owned eateries, I wasn't too familiar with it, but there were several cars in the parking lot, so I hoped that meant it was satisfactory. "Is this okay?" I asked when I pulled the SUV into a spot.

"This is great," he replied with excitement in his voice. Just then, his stomach growled loudly. He ducked his head in embarrassment as he unbuckled and pulled my coat tighter around him. "Sorry."

"Don't be," I answered gently. "I'm quite hungry myself." Waves of appreciation rolled off of Falcon as he reached for the door handle. I quickly exited the car and came around to his side, but he was already on the ground and shutting his door before I could help him. I offered him my elbow, greedy for any touch I could get. "Shall we?" He chewed on his lip for a moment before wrapping his hand around my arm and nodding. Even through my suit, I felt the tingle that came from contact with my mate. My pulse raced and my breathing quickened, but I worked hard to keep my appearance unflustered as we strolled inside.

We were told to sit anywhere we liked, so I escorted Falcon to a table in the back corner and pulled out his chair for him. He gave another shy smile as he took his seat and I sat across from him.

"What do you want to drink?" was barked from beside us. I looked up to see a middle-aged woman, staring at us like we were wasting her time by breathing.

"May I see a wine list?" I asked. The woman rolled her eyes and loudly popped a bubble with her chewing gum.

"We've got warm bottled beer and fountain soda."

I concluded that we were not dealing with the employee of the month. "Water is fine for me." She grunted and looked to Falcon.

"I'll take a Coke please." The woman tossed two menus on the table and left. Even her terrible disposition couldn't damper my mood; I was here with my beloved, and that meant more to me than anything.

I smiled as I watched Falcon hungrily peruse the menu. "Do you know what you'd like to eat?"

"I'm not sure," he answered without lifting his eyes. "Everything looks so good."

"Then that's what we'll order," I shrugged. Finally, he looked up at me with rounded eyes.

"Are you serious?"

"Why not? We're both hungry." He opened his mouth to protest, but I continued, "I insist. I'll order and I ask that you please honor me by eating your fill. Whatever we don't finish here, we can save until later."

"Thank you," Falcon whispered. He cleared his throat and averted his eyes from me. "You can take the leftovers with you, though," he added quietly. "I can't take them home with me."

I was relieved to learn my mate had a home, though I was sure it was an unfit one. "May I ask why?"

"It's just not a good idea," he shrugged, looking at the table.

Before I could ask any more questions, the waitress reappeared and slid our drinks in front of us, sloshing some of the liquid out onto the table. *Charming.* "What do you want to eat?" she asked gruffly as she pulled a tablet of paper from a pocket on her apron.

Falcon looked to me and I winked at him, making his lips twitch up into a pretty smile. "We'll take one of each of the pasta entrees, a basket of bread, the largest order of chicken wings with an assortment of sauces and…" I looked to my beloved. "What toppings would you like on your pizza?"

"I like meat, if that's fine with you."

"One large pizza with every meat you have to offer." I collected our menus and handed them to the waitress, who stared grumpily at me.

"You have to actually pay for all of this, you know. If you're trying to pull a fast one, you can just go ahead and leave now."

I retrieved my wallet from my pocket and produced my black credit card for her to take. Her eyes widened. "I'll put your order in right away, sir," she said in a much friendlier tone. I was sure she was mentally calculating her tip on our huge bill as she sauntered away.

My attention was caught by Falcon taking a long drink of his soda and moaning. "Wow. I haven't had pop forever; I forgot how good it is." My heart swelled at providing him with something he enjoyed, even if it was a small thing. "I still can't believe you ordered *everything* though," he smiled. "What do you do to be able to afford handing over hundreds of dollars for a dinner date and then order the whole damn menu?"

I smiled at how forward he was being; pleased Falcon had interest in me, even if it was just curiosity. "I'm head of security for the Javier Corporation," I answered proudly.

"Dang, no wonder you make the big bucks; Javier Corp owns like half the freaking city," he answered with wide eyes. "That's really impressive, Bastian."

"Thank you." I puffed up with pride knowing I'd impressed my beloved. "I enjoy my work very much, and the founder of Javier Corp, Dante Javier, is my best friend. We've known each other since we were children."

"That's so cool. So I'm guessing from your name and accent that you're Spanish?"

"Indeed. You are very intelligent, Cielito."

"I wouldn't say that," he countered, dropping his head again.

"I would." Even though his face was turned away from me, I could make out the upturned corners of his mouth. "And yes, I grew up in Madrid, Spain. I've always been close to Dante, and when he came to

America to take over his family's businesses, he asked me to come along as his assistant and take control of his security measures."

The story was mostly true; Dante built his empire from the ground up, but given the ages we looked and how long the franchises had been in business, it was easier to say he'd taken over. Bankrolling his own business ventures made matters easier for him so that he didn't have to bother with banks and lenders, but as far as taxes and things of that nature, Dante was currently acting as his own great-grandson. Having a few members of our coven within the local court systems have been beneficial as well to keep things running smoothly.

"He must trust you a lot, then," Falcon pointed out and I smiled. "Are you and him…?" he didn't finish his question, but the uncertainty and jealousy rolling off of him completed his thought.

The fact that my mate was becoming jealous and territorial over me after such a short time made me happier than I can explain, but I wanted him to know he had nothing to fear. "No. Dante is married to my very good friend Ben, and I assure you my interest lies only with you."

"Your...interest?" he asked, excitement and confusion lacing the air.

It was time to make my intentions clear. *Damn, what was the word Dante used with Ben when they first met? Ah, yes!* "Yes. I want to be your boyfriend."

Falcon choked on the drink of soda he was taking when I spoke. I sprung from my chair and patted his back until he waved me off and wiped his mouth with a napkin. I took my seat again, nervously awaiting his answer.

"Trust me, you don't," he finally replied sadly. Just as I was opening my mouth to argue, he continued, "You saw what was happening in that alley earlier. You know what I am."

"Yes I do," I nodded. "I know you are strong and brave." He shook his head no but I kept going. "You *had* to be to survive your circumstances; circumstances I want nothing more than to understand and help you through. I know we don't know each other very well, but I want to. I want to know everything there is about you, and I will tell you anything you want to know about me. Please, Falcon; give me a chance."

✶✶✶✶✶

Milo

Guilt burned in the pit of my stomach every time Bastian used the fake name I told him. It was instinct to use it anytime someone asked for my name, but now I felt like an ass for giving it to Bastian. The man had shown me more kindness in less than an hour than I'd seen in my whole life. I couldn't tell him my real name now, though; that would just prove to him I was a liar. I was so many things, and none of them were good enough for the wonderful man who sat before me. I had to show him that; to make him understand how crazy his request to be my "boyfriend" was.

    Part of me didn't want to, though. I'd never had a boyfriend before. And for as many times as I'd been bent over and fucked senseless or had a dick crammed down my throat, this was my first date. The idea of having someone to care for me; of being with this huge, protective, sexy man sent a thrill through my body. But that was just me being selfish. He deserved so much more. I needed to lay out everything to him, so he could see it was best if he left me alone. Hopefully he would still let me eat with him first, though. I was *really* hungry.

"I ran away from home at seventeen," I started, wanting to get it all out there; Bastian deserved the truth. Maybe it would make up for my deceiving him so far. "My mom died when I was young, and my dad couldn't handle it. He turned into a drunken, abusive asshole. I think he turned all of his pain on me." I looked up into Bastian's eyes and saw sadness and understanding shining back at me. It was too hard to look at him for the next part, so I trained my eyes back on the table.

"I ended up on the streets until a group of guys discovered me. I thought they were helping me when they invited me into their place, but they just wanted to use me." I stopped when a growling sound pierced the air. When I looked up at Bastian, he cleared his throat and nodded for me to continue. I dropped my gaze again. "At first, I was their drug mule. Then a dealer. But I sucked at both. Long story short, I was roped into prostitution."

The table grew blurry before me as moisture filled my eyes. "I've done so many terrible things, Bastian. I've been with so many men. I'm dirty. I'm no good. I hate it, but I can't leave; they'll kill me if I do. They own me." I rolled up the sleeve of his warm coat to reveal the tattoo Jerome gave me in his kitchen. "This is all I am. This is all I'll ever be." I rolled the sleeve back down and used it to dab my eyes dry.

"Falcon, please look at me," Bastian requested softly. Another bolt of guilt shot through me as I did so. "That," he started, pointing at my now covered wrist, "Does not define you. It is not who or what you are. Like I said, you are strong and brave and smart. You are *not* the dirty, no good one; the men who used you and forced you to do these terrible things are. Not that what you did is terrible," he added quickly. "It doesn't matter to me what you've done. I hate that you've had to endure such hardships, but I hold no ill will toward you. You should hold none toward yourself either, Cielito."

His sweet words and soft voice were everything I ever needed; everything I hoped to one day hear, but knew I never deserved. As much as I dabbed and wiped, I couldn't stop new tears from dripping down my face. "I don't want to go back, Bastian," I sobbed. "They hurt me. They cut me and hit me and don't let me eat. The men they send me to hurt me too." I hated to break down like this; it was so unlike me. I'd learned to hold everything in and not show emotion in front of Jerome or his men, because they always made me pay for it. But something told me Bastian was different. His eyes weren't judgmental or cold; they were sympathetic and caring. I needed to release some of the pain inside. The dam broke and everything I'd held in for three years came tumbling out.

"The men don't care if they hurt me. They don't get me ready or help me out. They only want to get to their happy ending. Most of the time I can't go to the bathroom without bleeding and crying because it hurts so bad. Sometimes my throat gets sore and burns because men shove themselves inside without caring what damage they do to me. But I can't stop; I can't refuse to work, the men I live with will hit me. They always hit me. Once, I had a bad cold and asked Jerome if I could have an evening off because it was hard to breathe; especially when I had something down my throat and couldn't get air through my blocked nose. I promised to make twice as much money the next night, but he broke two of my fingers and said the next time I complained, it would be my whole arm. I'm scared for my life, but I can't get away. I can't do it anymore, Bastian. I'm terrified. Sometimes I think it'd be better if they *did* kill me, but I'm scared of that too. I...I..."

My words stopped when two strong arms wrapped around me. I'd been crying too hard to even notice Bastian rising from his seat. I leaned into him and sobbed as he stroked my hair and whispered soothing Spanish words into my ear. I'd known this man for such a short time, but had just spilled my sob story out to him and didn't regret it. I knew people around us were staring, but I couldn't stop. It felt so good to let everything out. It felt even better to have someone to listen.

Slowly, I was able to stop crying as a sense of peace and comfort bloomed in my chest. It was as if Bastian was pumping support straight into me with how tightly he held me. The feeling was warm and pleasant and allowed me to not only dry my face, but bring a small smile to my lips.

"Thank you for listening," I whispered. "I'm sorry I unloaded on you like that." Guilt tried to rise up again, but the peaceful feeling was too overpowering.

"Falcon, please know you can come to me with anything. You honor me with your trust." He squeezed me one last time before taking his seat across from me again. I was suddenly cold without his big body wrapped around me, but I was still at peace. "Now, I would like for you to please tell me where these men live so that I may kill them."

A surprised laugh bubbled out of me. As I looked upon Bastian's stony face, however, I realized he was serious. "I can't; *you* can't!" I insisted. "There are too many of them and they have enough weapons to blow you away. I can't let that happen to you. Promise me you won't look for them, Bastian." I reached across the table to take his hand and gave him a pleading look. "*Please* promise me."

Bastian's other hand folded on top of mine. "It's okay, Falcon," he said quietly. "I promise you." I let out a sigh of relief. "But if you won't let me take care of them myself, we need to go to the police."

"We can't do that either," I replied sadly. "I know for a fact at least one cop is in business with Jerome. In fact, he was the first one I had to…" I couldn't finish my sentence, but the way Bastian's jaw clenched as he swallowed hard, I knew he understood. "I'm sorry; I didn't mean to upset you."

"I'm not upset with you, Cielito; never with you. I'm furious at the police officer who did not honor his oath to keep you safe." He squeezed my hand. "But *I* will keep you safe. I don't want you to go back to those terrible men. I would like for you to come home with me so that I may protect you. I will provide you with everything you need and desire. I promise you will never want for anything. Please, Falcon; you would be granting me the highest honor if you allow me this."

I didn't know what to say. Getting away from Jerome and his crew was everything I ever dreamed of and Bastian was promising that and so much more. He even acted like *I'd* be doing *him* a favor if I let him take me in. It was a risk, but what did I have to lose? My dirty cot shoved in a tiny closet? More broken bones? This evening with Bastian was better than any other in my entire life. Sure, he could turn crazy on me and hack me up in my sleep, but something deep inside me said I could trust him. Surely I could trust him more than Jerome. Granted, I wasn't exactly the king of good decisions, but this was my way out when I saw no other. I just hated that it felt like I was using this wonderful man. I had nothing to offer him. Unless…

"So, are you looking for a sugar daddy situation?" I asked. I didn't deserve to be his boyfriend; I was no good as a partner, but maybe I could be an okay sugar baby. I'd learned lots of tricks to make him happy.

Hell, just not getting passed around to everyone in town sounded like a dream come true.

Bastian cocked his head to the side in confusion. "I'm not familiar with the term."

Really? Maybe they didn't have such things in Spain. "Basically, a sugar daddy provides for someone financially, takes care of them and keeps them happy in exchange for their...*company*."

"That sounds lovely," Bastian smiled widely. "I want to provide and care for you and I enjoy your company very much."

Now *I* was confused; Bastian and I hadn't even...*Oh my god. He actually means just being in my company.* I didn't know whether to laugh or cry. I settled on saying, "I enjoy your company too, Bastian."

Bastian raised his glass. "Sugar daddies then?" he asked hopefully and I had to cough to cover up a laugh. The sweet man had no idea what I was talking about and it warmed my heart.

"Deal." I tapped my glass to his and Bastian smiled so widely, I thought his face might rip.

Just then, Suzie Sunshine came back to our table holding Bastian's credit card and a clipboard. "Your food will be out shortly," she said in a much sweeter tone than she'd used all night. "But I went ahead and ran your ticket. Your meal *was* all on one bill, right?"

"Yes," Bastian replied as he took his card and signed his name on the slip of paper attached to the clipboard after adding a *very* generous tip. He gave me a large smile before turning it on our waitress and announcing proudly, "I'm his sugar daddy."

The waitress's eyes grew large at his words and I lost it. I laughed long and loud and once I started, I couldn't stop. Poor Bastian appeared utterly confused. The woman looked at us both like we were crazy and slowly backed away, making me laugh even harder. It was something I hadn't done in years and I almost didn't recognize the sound coming out of my own body. The light, bubbly feeling that overtook me was foreign but wonderful.

Once I finally got myself under control and wiped away the tears that came with my fit of hysteria, I found Bastian looking at me with a dreamy grin. "You have a beautiful laugh, Cielito."

"Thank you," I answered shyly before tipping my head to the side. "What does that mean? Cielito?"

Bastian's goofy grin widened as he took my hand. "It means 'little sky' or 'little heaven', but to me, it means both." That cleared nothing up, and apparently Bastian could see my confusion, because he continued, "You are my heaven, Falcon; everything I've been waiting for my entire life, and more than I shall ever deserve. Now that we are together and sugar daddies, I will do everything I can to make your existence heaven on earth." I couldn't even laugh at his misuse of the term because I was so enthralled by his beautiful words.

"And I am enchanted by your eyes," he continued. "They are the color of the sky at my favorite time of day, when the sun gives way to dusk. They give me peace and comfort and hope. That is what you are to me, Cielito; my heaven, my sky, my everything."

Holy. Shit. My heart was about to beat out of my chest. Bastian's words were the most touching thing I'd ever heard, and what's more was that I believed him. This wasn't one of my clients calling me 'baby' because they didn't want to know my name. Bastian had put so much thought and sentiment into the endearment. And there was no teasing in his voice when he explained it. He wasn't blowing smoke up my ass or trying to flatter me; that was how he felt about me. My emotions were almost too much to process; I was grateful to the universe for putting this man in my path, confused about how he could see me in this light, and had affection brewing inside me like I'd never felt.

Bastian didn't press when I didn't say anything. He simply raised my hand to kiss the backs of my knuckles before placing it back on the table. He squeezed it gently and caressed his thumb over my skin.

"Here we go, guys," our waitress said when she approached our table again. She was carrying our pizza and had another waiter trailing her, hefting a large tray full of the multiple entrees Bastian ordered. Once they squeezed everything onto our table, they left quickly. I smiled as I wondered if our waitress told the other employees about what Bastian had said.

I smiled wider as I watched Bastian grab a plate from the end of the table and pile it high with a little of everything. Earlier, he said he was hungry and I guess he wasn't kidding. I couldn't blame him; the buffet spread out before us looked amazing and smelled even better. It was more food than I'd eaten in the past six months combined and I couldn't wait to dig in.

Before I could grab my own plate, however, Bastian reached across the table to set the food mountain he'd created in front of me. "I hope you enjoy it," he grinned, "And please let me know when you're ready for more."

I blinked at him before looking down at my plate, which was heaping full of pizza, pasta, chicken and bread. *The man served me food; before he even served himself!* Never in my life had someone put my needs before theirs. Sure, it was just a dinner plate, but it meant so much to me. I raised my head to thank him, but was unsure exactly what to say. Bastian simply winked at me and grabbed the other empty plate.

I made a complete pig of myself. I scarfed down my food like I hadn't eaten in a month, which wasn't that far from the truth. Bastian didn't seem to mind my less than perfect table manners, though. He just smiled as he watched me destroy helping after helping. And despite what he said, there was no 'letting him know when I was ready for more'. As soon as he noticed I finished off a portion, Bastian piled more onto my plate.

After three rounds of *everything*, I couldn't eat another bite. My belly felt as if it were about to pop, and I was having trouble even holding my head up. I laid it against the wall and smiled at the gorgeous man across the table.

"Would you like me to ask for a dessert menu?" he asked.

"Bastian, I can't," I moaned. "I'm already about to slip into a food coma." His eyes grew concerned as he quickly looked me over, making me chuckle again. Apparently sarcasm and slang phrases weren't his strong point, which I found adorable. "I'm only teasing. I just meant I'm very full." His features relaxed and I heaved my head up from the wall and reached out to lay my hand on top of his. "It was delicious, Papi. Thank you." I bit my lip, waiting for his reaction to the pet name.

I wanted to give him one since he had such a special name for me, and I knew I had to make his special too. This was nothing like the emotionless 'honey' I called my clients. I thought about this name the entire meal. I chose it because it was Spanish (I remembered it from my high school days), which I thought Bastian would appreciate, and because it meant 'Daddy', a nod to his 'sugar daddy' status that he seemed so proud of.

I didn't have to wait long for his reaction. Bastian's face exploded into a toothy grin as he sat up straighter and visibly puffed up with pride. I chuckled at how such a simple name turned the titan before me into a cheesing dork; a huge, intimidating, sexy cheesing dork, but still.

Bastian requested several boxes from our waitress and packed away all of our leftovers, waving me off when I offered to help. He took pleasure in caring for me and damn if it didn't make me feel special.

"Okay, I think that's everything," he said, giving the table another once-over. "Are you ready to go home?"

Home. Not to a dirty cot in a closet. Not to judgemental eyes and iron fists. The kindest man I'd ever met was inviting me into his home. Was I ready for that? Was I ready to leave this life behind and start a new chapter with a man who would protect me, care for me, and, if this night were any indication, spoil me rotten? Could I walk away from an admittedly terrible existence for something entirely unknown?

"Hell yes."

Chapter Two

Milo

I held my breath as Bastian and I stepped off the elevator that led to his apartment. I wasn't sure what to expect, but if it was anything like the rest of the building, I had a feeling my socks were about to get knocked off. Well, if I had socks. On my feet was just a pair of beat up old sneakers whose sole flapped up and down when I walked.

But back to the building; it was amazing! Bastian took me on a quick tour when we arrived, showing me a dance club (that I was too nervous to enter), a cafeteria (filled with all of the *free* food I could possibly eat!) and a medical wing, which provided free medical care. I couldn't believe such a place even existed.

And the people seemed great too. Nobody we passed looked down their nose at me, and all of them stood straighter at Bastian's presence, giving him the respect he deserved. The only person I actually met on the way up was one of Bastian's friends named Dmitiri. He was standing guard by the elevator and was very nice. He even called me sir! *Me!*

Bastian juggled the leftover food (which he wouldn't let me help carry) in one hand and unlocked his door with the other. "Welcome home," he crooned before pushing the door open and motioning me inside.

I stepped through the entrance and my jaw dropped. His living room was huge. It had charcoal gray flooring, white furniture, and teal rugs throughout. Circular silver lamps hung from the ceiling; the area was classic, cool and modern all at once. But the show stoppers were the large floor to ceiling windows that overlooked the city. My breath caught as I looked out over all of the twinkling lights.

"Your home is beautiful," I whispered in awe.

"It's your home too, Cielito," Bastian replied. He gave me a heart stopping smile as he motioned to the far side of the room. "May I show you the rest?"

"Please." I followed him into the kitchen, where he stored our leftovers in his large stainless steel fridge. The room was decorated in silver, black and dark brown. "It's gorgeous in here," I gushed, running my fingertips along the black and brown speckled countertop. "Do you like to cook?"

"I do," he answered with another smile. "Though my skills pale in comparison to my friend Ben's. He is a master in the kitchen." A small flicker of jealousy burned in my gut at his words. I never learned to cook, so it was something this *Ben* could offer Bastian that I couldn't and I didn't like it.

Even though Bastian told me earlier that Ben was a married man, I was still uneasy with the way Bastian spoke about him. Besides, I'd serviced enough married men to know that it didn't always matter. "I think you'd like Ben," Bastian continued in a placating tone, as if he could read my mind. "I would very much like to introduce you."

"I'm not sure I *want* to meet this *kitchen master*," I snipped. I crossed my arms over my chest when realization dawned on me. "Wait, you want me to meet your friends?" My heart leapt; I'd met Dmitri because he was manning the elevator and it was sort of unavoidable, but the fact that Bastian wanted to introduce me to everyone showed he didn't want to keep me secret and didn't seem ashamed of me.

"Of course I do," he answered gently, appearing hurt. "My greatest wish is for your happiness. I would love for you all to meet and become friends as well, so that you can have as much support and companionship as possible. But if you do not wish to meet them, I understand. They are a very important part of my life, but you are the *most* important person in my life."

Guilt took the place of jealousy in my stomach. Not only had I judged Bastian's friend without even meeting him, I'd disrespected Bastian in the process when he'd only been kind to me. It would take time, but I needed to learn to trust him. And I wouldn't be the one who separated him from his friends.

"I'm sorry for being rude," I whispered. "This is all new to me and..."

"I understand," Bastian interrupted. "Truly, I do. And I will never push you into anything you're not ready for."

"Thank you," I replied quietly. "But...I'd like to meet them. If it's important to you, it's important to me too."

"Thank *you,* Cielito. You don't know what this means to me." He combed his fingers through my hair, tucking it behind my ear while I had to hold in a moan. Bastian removed his hand and looked at it with squinted eyes. "Your hair is a little wet. Are you getting too warm in that heavy coat?"

It was grease he felt, not sweat, but I wasn't about to tell him that; it was too embarrassing. "A little," I lied. I was actually quite comfortable. Bastian was quick to remove the coat and fold it over the back of a chair. "Thanks for letting me borrow it."

"It's yours if you want it, but I'd rather get you one that fits you better so that it's more comfortable." Bastian's eyes lit up as he smiled. "Tomorrow afternoon I have some business to attend to, but perhaps tomorrow morning you would allow me to take you shopping for a new wardrobe?"

He looked so excited to spend money on me, how could I say no? And honestly, I needed clothes. All I had was the outfit on my back, and it was barely holding together. "That sounds amazing, Papi. Thank you."

Bastian's smile widened. "Anything for you." He took my hand and kissed the back of my knuckles.

"It's none of my business, but can I ask what you have to do tomorrow afternoon?"

"You can always ask me anything," he insisted. "I must escort Dante downtown to finalize the purchase of a business he's acquiring. It's a bookstore called *Page Turners*. You are welcome to come with me if-"

Bastian stopped speaking as I shook my head forcefully. I knew *Page Turners*; it was close to where I worked, and close to where Jerome lived. Close to where Bastian found me. "I can't go, Bastian. I can't. They live close and might see me. If they catch me-"

"Easy, Cielito," Bastian crooned, once again wrapping me in his warm embrace. His body was hard against mine, but still comforting; like a reminder of his strength, but that he had a tender side only for me. "It was only an idea. You are welcome to stay here." He backed away to look at me, a gentle smile on his face. "Perhaps I could ask Ben and his friend/bodyguard Sam to keep you company while I'm gone."

I didn't like the idea of being alone with strangers; I *especially* didn't like the idea of being alone with a huge, intimidating bodyguard, but I didn't want to upset Bastian again. Besides, I understood why he wouldn't want me in his apartment alone; he had to protect his belongings and property, though I would never steal from him.

"It's something to think about," he added, as if he could sense my unease. "For now, would you like to continue our tour?" I nodded, grateful for the distraction. He showed me a huge wardrobe filled with more suits than I thought any one person could possibly need, along with several pairs of jeans and dress shirts. He said the free half of the closet was for everything he was going to buy me to wear, which put a wide grin on my face.

He then pointed out a hall bathroom, which he claimed to be unexciting. He couldn't have been more wrong. It was big and nicely decorated, but that wasn't what got my pulse racing; it was the sight of a huge shower I hoped Bastian would let me use. Once a week, Jerome allowed me five minutes with two washcloths to keep down odors that could potentially turn away clients, but I craved a long hot shower. It looked like Bastian even had his bathroom stocked with bottles of soap! Maybe he wouldn't care if I used a little to freshen up.

"This is my favorite room of the house," Bastian announced as he stopped in front of a door in the hallway. "I hope it will be one of yours as well." He opened the door and my eyes widened at the sight of a home theater, filled with a long black leather couch and two matching recliners that looked very fancy, judging by the remote controls attached to them. All of the furniture was pointing to the far wall, which held a massive projector screen. "I must admit movies are a pleasure of mine. Do you enjoy watching movies, Falcon?"

I hadn't seen a movie since I'd been with Jerome, but I loved them. "Scary movies are my favorite," I told him, and a grin broke out over his face.

"Follow me!" he said excitedly before ushering me over to a cabinet in the corner. He opened it to reveal hundreds of DVDs, most of them of scary movies, from old black and white films to ones that looked brand new, though I didn't recognize the titles. "They're my favorite too. Maybe we could watch some together. Would you like to watch one tonight?" Seeing this big man looking like a kid in a candy store made me smile. As much as I loved movies and wanted to watch my first one in years, I was tired from the stress of the night and the big meal Bastian fed me and didn't think I could make it through a whole film. I couldn't stand the thought of disappointing him, though.

"I'd love to watch one with you," I answered in my most convincing tone.

Bastian's eyes narrowed a little. "Cielito, if you'd rather not, that's completely fine. I only offered because I thought it might make you happy."

Okay, apparently my convincing tone was crap. After only knowing me for a few hours, this man could read me like a book, which was both scary and exhilarating. "I'm a little tired," I replied truthfully. "I'm sorry; I didn't want to upset you. I appreciate you showing me this room and offering me your movies. I *really* want to watch some with you, but I also don't want to fall asleep and you think I don't like it or like what you're doing for me and-"

"Falcon, please look at me," Bastian urged in a gentle voice. I raised my gaze from the floor to look into his gorgeous cinnamon eyes. "I will *never* be upset with you for telling me your needs. I *want* to know them; I want to fulfill them. Never think you have to do something to make me happy; you make me happy by just being here with me. It doesn't matter what we do. I'm here for anything you want or need. Do you understand?" I understood *what* he was saying, but not why. I decided not to question it, but just to accept it with a grateful heart. I nodded and Bastian smiled. "If you're tired, I would be happy to show you to your sleeping quarters. Is there anything else you need right now?"

I hated to ask for anything more than this wonderful man was already offering, but I did have a pressing need; a need that was making my scalp itch and my nose twitch. "Could I please take a shower?" I asked shyly. "I'll be very quick."

"Oh, Cielito," Bastian sighed, giving me a sad smile. "Please come with me." He led me back down the hall but didn't stop at the bathroom he showed me earlier. Instead, he opened another door and we stepped into a large bedroom, complete with a dark brown king sized bed dressed in teal covers, a dark brown dresser and nightstand, and a big TV on the wall across from the bed. "This is your bedroom. I hope you will find it comfortable and pleasant."

He'd shown me every other room in his place, and this was the only one that held a bed. "Bastian, is this *your* room?"

Excitement and a little fear warred in my stomach over sharing the space with him. He'd been nothing but a gentleman so far, which was both a relief and a frustration. Usually "sugar daddies" expected certain things from their companions, but Bastian hadn't mentioned anything like that. Maybe he wasn't interested in that sort of thing. On the other hand, he *did* say he wanted to be my boyfriend and that I was gorgeous. I was confused to say the least. It was nice to have someone who didn't demand sexual favors from me, but I *liked* Bastian. And he was the only man in years to excite me in a physical way; my body usually didn't react to men anymore. Sex became a chore and a burden, but I couldn't deny being curious and hopeful when it came to the sexy man standing next to me.

"I will sleep in the theater," he shrugged. I shook my head no, but he held up a hand. "Truly, it's no trouble. The sofa is very comfortable. I've fallen asleep there many times."

"I'll take the sofa," I argued. "You've done so much for me, Bastian; I don't want to take your bed. The couch is more than I need; more than I deserve."

Bastian cupped my cheeks in his hands. "You deserve the world, Falcon. Please allow me this; I want you to be warm and comfortable." What could I say? I couldn't find words at all, so I just nodded, bringing a smile to Bastian's lips. "Thank you. Now, you're welcome to either bathroom, of course, but this one is much nicer." He led me through a door on the far side of the room which led into a second bathroom. This one was even larger, and the same could be said for the shower inside. It had a seat in it and three different nozzles. I nearly vibrated with excitement.

"There is soap, shampoo and conditioner in the shower," Bastian explained as he kneeled on the floor. "And let me get you anything else you may need." He rifled through a cabinet and set several items on the counter before standing. "Here we are; shaving cream, a razor, loofah, and a toothbrush and toothpaste. Is there anything else you can think - *oof!*" His last words were squashed as I slammed my body into him for a fierce hug. I was so overwhelmed with gratitude and happiness, I didn't know what else to do.

"Thank you, Papi. Thank you so much for everything." Bastian hugged me back and dropped a gentle kiss to the top of my dirty hair. My eyes stung with unshed tears.

"You're so welcome," he replied softly. "It brings me such joy to see you happy." After one more kiss, he released me. "Please take as long as you wish in the shower; there is no need to rush. Relax and enjoy. If you leave your clothing on the bed, I will send them off for cleaning. I will place some of my clothes on the bed for you to wear for pajamas after your shower, unless you would like me to ask Ben if he has something you could borrow. I'm sure he won't mind and he is closer to your size."

Hearing one of Bastian's friends was small like me gave me a huge amount of relief. Bastian's size didn't scare me because I now knew the man and the kindness within him, but knowing I wouldn't be totally surrounded by other large men was nice. That didn't mean, however, I wanted to wear the other small man's clothes. I was already inconveniencing Bastian; no need to trouble his friends. "No, don't bother him," I said, shaking my head.

"It's no bother, Cielito," Bastian insisted.

"Can I be honest with you?" I asked, dropping my gaze to my feet. Bastian was having none of it and placed a finger under my chin until I raised my head to look at him.

"Always; no matter what you need to tell me, I will not be upset. I swear it."

"I...I like the idea of wearing your clothes." I'd never had the opportunity to steal a sweatshirt from a boyfriend to wrap up in and remind me of him. Wearing something of Bastian's excited me in a way that now, saying it aloud, seemed silly. My eyes trailed from his down to his mouth, which curled up into a sweet smile.

"I like it too, Falcon." He pressed his lips to my forehead and I actually sighed with happiness. Now that Bastian was becoming more affectionate, I wanted, no *needed* more. His gentle words and caring touches were like nothing I'd ever experienced. "I will leave you to your shower," he smiled. "I'll come back into the bedroom in a few minutes to collect your clothing and leave you some of mine. Please take your time and enjoy, Cielito."

With that, he tucked my hair behind my ear again and left me alone in the bathroom. I was quick to strip off my disgusting clothes and lay them on the floor beside the bed in the adjoining room; they were too dirty to put directly on Bastian's nice blankets. I'd rather he throw them away instead of having them cleaned, but knew I'd need something to wear to go shopping tomorrow. As much as I wanted to wear Bastian's clothes, I'd probably look ridiculous wearing his much larger things in public.

The shower was absolute heaven. I turned the water as hot as I could stand it and scrubbed my body three times with the loofah Bastian gave me. His soap smelled woodsy and dark, and was one of the best scents I'd ever encountered. I washed my hair several times as well, hoping to cleanse all the grease away. I didn't need the razor

Bastian gave me, as I'd never been able to grow a beard and had little body hair to speak of, but I appreciated it just the same.

I have no clue how long I spent in that shower, but when I emerged, the mirror was fogged and I felt better than I could ever remember. I was clean, relaxed and warm. I dried off my body and shaggy hair before hanging up the towel and brushing my teeth. I peeked into the bedroom. Bastian wasn't there and the door to the hallway was closed, so I walked over to the pile of fresh clothes on the bed.

I pulled a plain white t-shirt on over my head and laughed at the way it fell to my knees. Next, I stepped into a pair of boxers Bastian left for me. It sent a naughty thrill through my body to be wearing his underwear. Or...*attempting* to wear his underwear, anyway. When I pulled them onto my hips, they immediately fell to the ground again. I had no meat on my body to hold them up. The same was true for the pair of sleep pants he loaned to me.

I folded the bottoms neatly and carried them out into the hall. I felt a bit exposed just wearing Bastian's long t-shirt, but everything was covered. I didn't see him in the kitchen or living room, so I went looking for him in the home theater. *I can't believe I'm staying in a house with a home theater.* The door was open, so I walked inside. My breath caught at what I saw.

Bastian was getting the sofa prepared for sleep, placing a pillow and blanket on the cushions. His hair was wet and his skin was flushed, I assumed from a shower of his own, and he was dressed only in a pair of low-slung gray sleep pants. I was pleasantly surprised to see there wasn't a cut on his abdomen from the knife earlier; the thick material of his suit must have blocked the blade from getting to his skin.

I moved my eyes hungrily over Bastian's body. It was smooth, thick and chiseled; slabs of muscle separated by deep ridges covered every delicious inch I could see. And talk about inches. He was apparently not wearing underwear, and though he was soft, I could make out the outline of his huge penis through his thin cotton pants.

"Did you enjoy your shower, Cielito?"

At the sound of Bastian's voice, I squeaked and dropped the clothes I was holding. I also snapped my gaze from the python in his pants to his amused grin. "Yes, thank you. I...I'm sorry to bother you. I, um...I brought these back to you." In a fluster, I picked up the pants and underwear and held them out to Bastian. "They're too big, but thank you." Bastian's eyes grew dark as they roved over my body dressed only in his shirt. My own *non*-python sized dick twitched under his perusal. I shifted my legs, making sure nothing poked out the front.

"It's no bother at all," he answered in a husky voice before clearing his throat. "I always enjoy seeing you. I'm sorry the clothes didn't work out for you; I can try to find something smaller if you like."

"No, I'm fine in this, but thank you." He took the pants from my hands and gave me a warm smile. "Well, I guess I'll be going to bed now."

"May I tuck you in?"

My heart nearly burst from my chest because of his sweet words and the hopeful way he asked them. I nodded and his grin grew wider. He sat the clothing he held on the sofa and led me back to the bedroom with a hand on the small of my back. It was an innocent touch that had my blood boiling. I'd be glad to get under the blanket because it was becoming harder to keep anything from poking out.

Bastian pulled the covers down by the corner and motioned for me to climb into bed. I did so, cradling my head on the pillow and sighing. The mattress was plush beneath me and the pillow supported my head perfectly. It was a million times better than my cot. Bastian tucked the blankets around me and I was surrounded by a warm cocoon. I was pretty sure this is what heaven felt like. And I was positive the beautiful man taking care of me was what it looked like.

"Do you need anything else before I retire?" Bastian asked, smoothing the blankets over my chest. "Anything at all I can do to make you more comfortable or bring you pleasure?"

My dick twitched again at the thought of Bastian giving me pleasure. I knew that wasn't what he meant, but I couldn't stop my brain from going there. I hadn't been interested in sex for so long, having decided long ago it would never be anything I'd enjoy. None of the greedy bastards I serviced ever did anything to give me pleasure. When I first started the work Jerome forced me to do, I couldn't stop my body from physically reacting even though nobody ever tried to make me feel good. Soon enough, my body lost all interest and the only thing I got from the encounters was pain. I hadn't had release in so long, and I couldn't deny it was something I now craved. Especially seeing the heat in Bastian's eyes as he watched me react to his innocent offer that I turned dirty.

"Would you like me to give you pleasure, Cielito?" he asked in a deep, raspy voice.

Oh god. There was no mistaking that offer. My heart beat wildly and I was fully hard beneath the covers. "I..." When my voice cracked, I swallowed and tried again, "I want nothing more than that, Papi, but...I'm a little sore...down there. I don't think I can do anything. I'm so sorry." I wanted to push through for him, but seeing how big he was earlier in a *soft* state, there was no way I could let him inside me tonight. I was afraid if I tore or cried or made it unpleasant for him in any way, he'd not want me any longer.

"Sweet Falcon, you misunderstand me," he crooned, trailing the backs of his fingers down my heated cheek. "I'm not looking for anything from you. Not that I don't desire your perfect little body or crave to be with you in such a way, but I would like to bring *you* pleasure if you will allow me. I want nothing in return."

Good lord, this man is too good to be true. "I would never ask you to do that, Bastian," I answered seriously. I never wanted to take advantage of him in any way.

"You're not asking; I'm offering," he insisted, combing his fingers through my hair. "I will never push you, nor ask you for anything you do not freely give. If this is something you don't want, I will happily bid you goodnight and leave you be, caring for you as strongly as I did before we came in. Whatever you desire, in this instance or any other, will never change the way I feel about you."

My eyes filled with tears. Not only was he professing he had some type of feelings for me, he was giving me the freedom of choice; the choice of whether I wanted him to pleasure me with no expectations. I swallowed hard and blinked away the moisture. "I...yes. Please, Papi. I...I want you to pleasure me." My cheeks burned at the admission, but not as strongly as Bastian's gaze as he sat on the side of the bed and leaned over me.

He caressed my cheeks with his thumbs as his eyes flicked over every inch of my face, as if trying to memorize it. He lowered his mouth to mine, but at the last second before he kissed me, I turned my head so that his lips pressed against my cheek.

"I'm sorry," I said quickly when he pulled back, giving me a look of confusion. "I don't kiss on the lips. I mean, I never have. A couple of times, a guy has forced his lips onto mine, but I've never kissed back. It has nothing to do with you," I added, hoping I wasn't hurting his feelings. "I *want* to kiss you. You're the first man I've ever wanted to kiss, but...I'm just nervous. I'm sorry. I probably sound so pathetic..."

Bastian shushed me gently with soothing sounds. "You are most certainly *not* pathetic, and please don't apologize. *I* apologize if I did anything to make you uncomfortable." I shook my head forcefully; I didn't want him to think he'd offended me. He smiled and his thumbs went back to their gentle caressing. "Is it okay if I kiss your body?"

"Hell yes."

Bastian laughed for the first time since I'd met him. It was a deep, booming sound that vibrated my chest and stole my heart. "Thank you." He bent toward me again, and again I ruined the moment.

"Wait!"

Bastian backed away, looking concerned but not angry. "Did you change your mind, Falcon? Because it's okay if you did. If at any point you wish for me to stop, just say the word."

If he hadn't already taken my heart, that sentence would have secured it as his. "No, it's not that. It's just...I'm not sure what you have planned, but...well, all of the condoms I had were in my jeans pocket. Oh god, and your money! I'm sorry Bastian, I forgot all about your money..."

"It's okay, Cielito," he soothed. "First of all, that was your money; I gave it to you and I want you to have it."

"No," I insisted. "It's yours. You took me out on such a nice date; my very first date. Please don't think you have to pay me for that."

"Our date was your first?" he asked, looking upset.

Oh god, what did I do? "Yes?" I answered in an unsure voice.

"I'm so sorry, Falcon; I would have taken you somewhere nicer if I'd known. I hope you allow me to make it up to you."

"Are you serious?" I asked in surprise. "I said I wanted pizza and you bought it for me; along with literally everything else on the menu, and you let me eat all I wanted! Then you brought me back to this beautiful home and let me take a hot shower. With soap! Papi, I can't imagine a better date than that."

"Oh, Cielito," he whispered, "You honor me." He kissed my cheek and smiled. "And as far as the money goes; yes, it's yours. I could never take back something I gave to you. I saw it peeking out of your pocket when I collected your clothing and I placed it here in the nightstand next to your bed. I hope you use it for something that will make you happy."

"*You* make me happy," I blurted, and Bastian grinned again.

"You make me happy too, Falcon. Happier than I ever thought possible."

Fuck it. I sat up in bed, took a deep breath, and smooshed my lips to Bastian's. He tensed in surprise for a moment before melting against me. He wrapped his arms loosely around my waist, allowing me room to escape if I wanted to. That only made me want to kiss him more. Everything he did made me want to kiss him; his sweet words, the respect he gave me...everything. I froze up at first from nerves, but there was never any doubt as to what I wanted.

Bastian didn't press to deepen our kiss, and neither did I; mainly because I wasn't sure what I was doing and didn't want to do anything to ruin our first kiss - *my* first kiss. Not that anything could ruin this; Bastian's lips were soft as they nibbled and pecked against mine. His fingers traced shapeless patterns on my lower back and his body heat seeped into me, warming me from the inside out. It was perfect.

When I finally released his lips, Bastian's eyes slowly opened. He looked at me so intensely, I would swear he could see my soul. "My heart is full," he whispered, and my stomach did a somersault. Bastian cupped my cheeks and placed a sweet kiss on the tip of my nose, making me smile. I lay back down, nestling into the covers again, warm and happy. The heat in Bastian's gaze reminded me of his offer that I'd forgotten in the bliss of our kiss. He leaned over me once more and gently kissed my cheek before trailing his lips down my neck.

I remembered something else I'd forgotten too. "The condoms?" I whispered, not wanting to interrupt him again.

"I threw them away," he whispered back and my body tensed. I'd never done anything without protection. "I didn't want any remaining tokens of your life before we met," he explained and my heart swelled. "I promise not to do anything without one that may make you uncomfortable." He kissed my neck again before raising his head to look into my eyes. "Do you trust me?"

"Yes," I answered easily. After only one night, I trusted this man more than I'd ever trusted anyone in my life.

*****

Bastian

Having my mate's trust filled me with more happiness than I thought my body could contain. Again and again tonight he was granting me with Fate's blessings; from allowing me to see to his needs to gracing me with his first kiss. I would never take that special gift for granted.

I eased the blanket down my beloved's body, lifting it over his feet and folding it onto the bottom of the bed. I smiled at the sight of his little toes; I couldn't wait to get my lips on them, but I didn't want to miss any of his delectable body parts on my way.

Falcon shivered at the loss of the cover, so I climbed over his beautiful body, keeping my weight off of him but allowing my heat to warm him. I stared into his mesmerizing eyes, stunned by the need and want shining in them. I planned on giving him everything he desired.

I lowered my face to his, but stopped as my lips hovered above his mouth. He kissed me once, but I did not want to take advantage or assume he wanted to kiss me again. I need not have worried, as Falcon eliminated the space between us and touched his lips to mine.

I sipped from his plush pillows, loving them gently with my teeth and lips. I wanted to sink my tongue into his mouth to taste his delicious flavor, but I also didn't want to push. Testing the waters, I peeked out my tongue and ran it slowly along the seam of his mouth. Falcon opened slightly and touched the tip of his slick appendage to mine. His naturally sweet, buttery flavor overpowered the toothpaste that clung to his skin. With that one small taste, I was addicted.

We slid our tongues together slowly, licking and exploring each other's mouths. Falcon carefully studied every surface of my cheeks, teeth and tongue with his. With every brush of our taste buds, he whimpered beautifully into my mouth, and I could actually taste the yearning on his breath.

I withdrew my tongue and kissed him soundly before pressing my lips to his neck. I nibbled and sucked the place I longed to sink my fangs; to claim my beloved for all time. His pulse beat rapidly beneath his skin, drawing my teeth down, but I moved on. I would never take from my mate without his permission.

"May I raise your shirt?" I asked breathlessly. Falcon surprised me by gripping the bottom hem of the fabric and pulling it free from his body. He lay it beside him in the bed and my mouth watered at the sight of my fully nude mate.

His skin was pale and taught over his thin frame. I could easily make out the bumps of his ribs and hip bones, along with the pretty blue map of his veins; the vessels that carried the life force that would sustain me forever. My eyes continued downward and I moaned when I saw his cock, standing tall and dripping as it pulsed. He was just under six inches long and average girth. His fuschia tip was circumcised and glistening.

The longer I stared at him, the more my mate's anxiety rose. I wanted to soothe any fears or doubts he may be feeling, so I lifted my eyes to his. "You are so incredibly beautiful, Cielito."

"Thank you," he whispered, before shyly adding, "So are you."

My mate's sweet compliment sent my heart soaring. I was beyond pleased he enjoyed the way I looked. I gently kissed his cheek and turned my attention back to worshipping his perfect little body. I nipped along his collar bone and traced my tongue along each line of his captivating tattoo. I loved the ink and wanted to know the meaning behind it, but didn't want to stop my ministrations to ask.

I trailed my tongue down his chest and stopped to circle one of his pretty pink nipples. Falcon moaned loudly as his flesh pebbled under my touch. I flicked my tongue quickly over the bead, and he rolled his head side to side in ecstasy. I caught his pointed nipple between my teeth and bit down gently, nibbling on his sensitive skin as he moaned again.

My beloved whimpered in protest when I released his flesh, but his whine turned into a moan as I kissed a line down his abdomen. I stopped to love on his hip the same way I did his nipple, circling it with my tongue before gingerly biting down on the protruding bone. When my lips reached his groin, Falcon's breathing was rapid and shallow.

When I kissed down his thigh instead of giving his weeping cock any attention, I got a frustrated groan from my mate, which made me smile. I intended on loving every inch of him; his patience would pay off. My lips pecked down Falcon's shin and ankle. When I got to his sweet little toes, I gave each of them a kiss before plunging his big toe into my mouth. My mate moaned and clutched at the sheets as I sucked the digit, laving it with my tongue.

After thoroughly enjoying his tasty toes, I crawled back up my mate's body, running my tongue up his opposite leg. This time, when I reached his inner thigh, I didn't stop. I licked a slow line across his fuzzy sack and Falcon's back arched off the bed as he swore at the ceiling. I wanted my beautiful mate to lose control. I slipped one of his tender orbs into my mouth and sucked gently.

"Oh, Bastian!" he cried, fisting the sheets tighter. "That feels amazing!"

I swirled my tongue through the sparse hair as I licked every inch of his sack. I sucked each of his testicles into my mouth and bounced them on my tongue. I nipped them gently and licked them thoroughly until Falcon was a trembling mass of moans and swear words. Before he could catch his breath, I swallowed his cock down to the root in one smooth motion.

"Papi!" he screamed, nearly flying off the bed. "Yes! Oh god, yes!"

I sucked hard, pulling every sweet drop that leaked from him into my mouth. I swirled my tongue around his tip, collecting his flavor before gobbling him back down again. When my lips were against the coarse hair of his base, I swallowed around him, massaging his hot flesh with my throat muscles. My beloved screamed and panted, humping further into my mouth. I relaxed my throat to take him in, eager to give him anything he needed.

"Oh Papi...Oh Bastian..." he chanted over and over as he thrust his hips back and forth. I sucked as hard as I could as he fucked my throat, providing him with slick, hot friction. "Papi, I'm getting close," he warned. I wanted nothing more than to suck him until he burst and drink down every delicious drop he gave me, but I promised him I wouldn't do anything without a condom that may make him nervous. And considering I hadn't told him I was immune to giving or receiving human diseases, I regrettably had to let his perfect cock fall from my lips.

I took his hard flesh in my hand and pumped my wrist quickly. Falcon propped his weight on his heels and thrust his hips off the bed. I took the opportunity to prop up on my knees and slide them under his thighs. While I continued to stroke him with one hand, I took his balls in my other and massaged them.

My hand was just a blur as I jacked my mate as fast as I could. I wasn't worried about him seeing my vampire speed because his eyes were screwed shut and his teeth were gnashed together.

"Dame todo, Cielito," I begged. "Give me everything!"

With a final cry, Falcon's cock engorged in my hand before exploding. His cum sprayed up the length of his body, painting him from chin to navel as he pulsed and released burst after burst of white, creamy liquid. I had to stop myself from leaning forward and licking up everything he gave.

My mate's body convulsed as his hips gave a few last thrusts into my hand. His breathing slowly changed from ragged gasps to a calm pattern and his eyes peeled open.

"Bastian, that was..." his eyes flicked between mine as he thought, but nothing came out.

"Perfect?" I offered, and my mate nodded. "*You're* perfect." I watched as his eyes clouded and a tear slipped down his cheek. I would be worried I pushed too far if it weren't for the overwhelming feelings of happiness and affection pouring from him.

"I'm sorry," he said, wiping his face quickly. "It's just...nobody's ever...I mean, I've never felt...I'm sorry," he repeated.

"Don't apologize, Cielito," I pleaded. I wiped away another tear as it fell from his eye before leaning down and giving his lips a soft, slow kiss. Now that he'd allowed me a taste, I would never get enough.

When I raised back up, Falcon chuckled. "Oops," he said, pointing to my stomach, where some of his release had rubbed onto me during our kiss.

"Believe me, this is the opposite of a problem," I countered, making him laugh again. "Let me go get something to clean you up; I'll be right back." I rose from the bed and Falcon gasped as his eyes landed on my groin. My pajama pants were tented away from my body by my hard, aching cock and a large wet spot darkened the fabric.

"Bastian, you made me feel so good," he whispered, still staring at my pelvis. "I can return the favor...if you want me to." My cock stiffened even more at his offer, but I took a seat beside him on the bed and gave him a gentle smile.

"Falcon, I meant it when I said I expected nothing in return."

"I know you don't; that's why I want to," he replied, his cheeks tinging pink. I had every intention of walking away and picking this conversation up on a night after my mate was settled in and comfortable, but my restraint broke when Falcon ran his hand up and down my thigh and looked and me pleadingly. "Please, Papi; I want to do this for you. I want to make you feel good."

*****

Milo

I meant it; I wanted this more than anything. I wanted to give him the same pleasure he'd given me, and not because I felt I needed to; I craved it. I wanted to see what it was like to willingly share this with someone I actually cared about.

Bastian swallowed thickly before asking, "You don't feel like you need to?" I shook my had no. "It's only because you want to?" I nodded. "And you know this has no bearing on how I feel about you?" I nodded again, too anxious and jittery to use words. "Then yes, Cielito, I would love to share this with you." He laughed as I clawed at the top of his sleep pants and quickly peeled them down. When I got a look at his firm cock, I certainly wasn't laughing.

I knew he was going to be big from the outline in his pants, but I wasn't prepared for what I found. His dick was nearly the size of my forearm in both length and girth. Sure, I was a relatively small guy, but *damn!* He had to be at *least* nine inches long. I was both proud that this beast was mine and a little scared for what the future might bring.

I wrapped my fingers around him and gave a slow stroke. Bastian drew a breath in through gritted teeth as his eyes slid closed. I continued to move slowly along his length, feeling each vein and ridge. I never got the chance to explore any of the men I'd touched before, nor did I want to. Bastian was different; I wanted to savor every moment with him.

I stroked up to his tip, where I stopped to collect a drop of pre-cum that leaked out of him, which I rubbed around his sensitive flesh with my thumb. I circled his slit, dipping my thumbnail inside.

"Tu toque lo es todo," Bastian moaned as I teased his tip. I loved hearing his sexy Spanish words, but wish I knew what they meant. This didn't seem like the time to ask, but his tone told me they were good. My right hand pumped his dick steadily while I brought my left one up to cup his balls. They were heavy and coated in coarse black hair that tickled my palm when I massaged them.

"I love the way that feels, Cielito," Bastian murmured, his voice thick with lust. I tightened my grip on his sack and pulled; not enough to hurt, only to pleasure. Judging by the way his head fell back on his shoulders as he moaned, I got it just right.

I rolled, squeezed and pulled his balls while I stroked his cock faster. A steady clear stream dripped down the side of his dick, slicking my path and helping me pump him even quicker. Bastian chanted words that I didn't understand, but instinctively knew were naughty.

"Falcon, you're going to make me come, beautiful." Those words were not only naughty, but welcome and sweet. No one had ever called me beautiful before Bastian, and he made me believe it; made me feel it. I tightened my grip and jacked him for all I was worth. My wrist burned as I stroked him feverishly, but I pressed on. I bounced his balls gently in my palm until they drew up close to his body.

A growl ripped from Bastian's chest as his cock erupted over my hand and onto my stomach, mixing with my own seed on my skin. I milked every last drop out of him until his breathing calmed and he softened in my hand. Even then I didn't want to let him go, but I reluctantly released him.

A satisfied grin crossed Bastian's lips as he opened his eyes. "That was incredible, Cielito; *you're* incredible." I leaned forward to kiss him and his smile widened. "*Now* I'll go get something to clean you up," he teased, and I chuckled. He stood up, kissed my lips again and tucked himself back into his pants before disappearing into the bathroom. He returned with a warm, wet cloth which he gently scrubbed over my chest and stomach.

"Thank you," I whispered. His care and tenderness filled my heart with warmth.

"You're welcome," Bastian said as he wiped the spunk from my chest. "I love your tattoo. May I ask what it means?"

I smiled down at the ink. I hated how I got it and what happened afterward, but I did love the design. "It stands for my longing for freedom; my wish to fly away from what held me." The same wish was also what sparked the name 'Falcon'.

"That's beautiful," he whispered.

"I never thought I'd get away," I told him seriously. "But then you came and you saved me. I can never thank you enough, Bastian. I don't know how I got so lucky, but I will be forever grateful for you."

"I'm the lucky one, Cielito," he countered before giving me a soft kiss. He wrapped his arms around me and I lay my head on his strong chest. The steady thump of his heartbeat and the gentle rise and fall of his breathing soothed me and soon, my eyelids grew heavy. I couldn't stop the yawn that overtook my lips. "Allow me to get you tucked back in," Bastian requested before helping me back into his shirt and smoothing the blankets around me when I lay down.

I wondered why he wasn't climbing into bed with me, especially after what just happened between us. I figured it was for my comfort or to give me time to wrap my head around everything. Truth was, I would like him to climb in with me, but I was afraid to ask him in case *he* needed space.

Bastian leaned down to give me a sweet kiss before combing my hair from my forehead. "Sleep well, Falcon."

My stomach knotted up with guilt for the hundredth time tonight. I wanted to tell him my name, but didn't want to risk upsetting him with my dishonesty after the beautiful moment we had together.

"Goodnight, Bastian."

He closed the door behind him as he disappeared into the hall. I snuggled down into the soft bed and once again felt my eyes grow heavy. I slipped into sleep easily, praying I didn't wake up to find this evening had just been a wonderful dream.

Chapter Three

Bastian

After I got my mate settled in bed and heard his breathing even out from the other side of the bedroom door, I called my friends for an emergency meeting. I couldn't wait to fill them in on finding my beloved. I only contacted Dante, Ben and Sam, as Dmitri had already met Falcon earlier and congratulated me in a vampire whisper. Plus, Dmitri's shift was over and I knew he would be spending time with his mate Sondra. The two of them met when Sondra transferred to our coven after the mess with Hugo was cleared up. We were all (including Dmitri) surprised to discover his mate was female, but gender did not matter to him. Fate's pairings were always perfect. Dmitri and

Sondra fell in love instantly, and bonded before the coven in a lovely ceremony the very next day.

I'd just stepped into the clean pajama bottoms that didn't fit Falcon (I didn't want to greet my company with a cum stain on my pants) when a knock sounded at my door.

I opened the door and smiled at the sight of Dante carrying a very sleepy-looking Ben, who clung to his husband like a baby koala. It wasn't *that* late, but I knew I'd woken the little sweetie up. Even if I *didn't* know Ben couldn't make himself stay up late, his outfit gave him away. He was wearing one of Dante's t-shirts, and though I couldn't see any bottoms, I was sure he was at least wearing underwear, as his protective mate would never let him around other men without them.

Dante was wearing a pair of sweatpants; they and the t-shirts he owned were all new additions to his wardrobe since he'd met his beloved. He cuddled Ben close to him, nuzzling his cheek over his lover's head. The man was a force to be reckoned with, but turned into a mushy romantic at the hands of his man.

"We came as soon as we could," my friend said seriously, but I just smirked. I was sure there was at least *some* dressing involved before they left their apartment, which was on the floor above mine. "What's wrong, Bastian?"

Before I could answer him, Sam strolled in through my open door, wearing only a pair of athletic shorts. His light blond hair was in disarray and his face was flushed.

"This had better be a real emergency," he barked. "I left two very sexy, *very* horny men in my apartment. And I don't want them to finish without me, so if we could wrap this up quickly, that'd be great." I could tell from his disheveled appearance and the way his shorts tented away from his body I'd taken him from a good time, but I couldn't find it in me to care. The news of my mate was more important. Besides, it wasn't like Sam was hurting for company.

I stood tall and smiled at my friends. "I found my mate."

Ben came alive in Dante's arms, twirling around to see me. "Bastian, that's wonderful!" The little man launched himself into my embrace. Full of happiness, I laughed and spun him around in a circle.

"This is indeed happy news, old friend," Dante added, holding his hand out for me to shake. When I did, he pulled me into a one armed hug before plucking his husband from my hold and snuggling him close again.

Even Sam smiled at me. "What's the lucky bastard's name?"

"I don't know," I answered honestly.

"Well, this has been fun," Sam said with an eye roll. "I'm going back to the big dick duo." When he stepped toward my door, Dante gripped him by the back of the neck and spun him around to face me. "You know, you wouldn't choke me so much if you knew how much I like it."

A growl sounded in Dante's chest, and to my surprise, one came from Ben as well. "Babe, did you just growl at me?" Sam asked with a wide smile. "That was the cutest thing I've ever heard!"

"It wasn't supposed to be *cute*," Ben pouted. "It was supposed to be scary."

"Scary as a newborn puppy," Sam teased. Dante slapped the back of his head, but Ben paid him no mind. He was too busy giving sad eyes to his husband.

"*You* think I'm scary, right, osito?"

"I think you are everything." The couple began kissing passionately, groping and pawing at one another.

"Oh for fuck's sake," Sam grumbled with another eye roll. He turned his attention back to me. "So, what the hell do you mean you don't know your mate's name? Did you just see him from a distance or something?"

"No, I met him. He's here in my bedroom," I answered proudly.

"You don't even know his name, but..." Sam's eyes widened. "Holy shit, did you *kidnap* him?"

"Of course not!" I replied indignantly. "I would never treat my mate with such disrespect!"

"Don't get your nuts in a knot, it was just a question," he shrugged.

"He's here?" Ben asked, finally catching up to the conversation once he peeled his lips from Dante's. "Oh, can we meet him? *Please*?" He bounced on his toes and clapped his hands.

"I'm sorry, but he's resting right now," I told Ben, who visibly deflated. "He had a very tiring night."

"I bet he did," Sam smirked, bouncing his brows. "At least he and I have something in common, huh?" The way he nudged my side with his elbow and continued to make his brows dance said he was speaking of our previous trysts.

"Sam, that is one reason I asked you here tonight. I implore you to not mention our past...*encounters* to my mate."

"Why?" he asked seriously. "They didn't mean anything." His face twisted up into an evil grin. "Unless...are you secretly in love with me?" Ben gasped and covered his mouth while Sam held his arms out and puckered his lips at me. "Oh, Bastian! If I'd only known you felt the same way, I never would have let those two men downstairs put their monster dicks anywhere near my hole!"

"Get away from me." I swatted at him as he burst into laughter. Ben relaxed once he realized this was one of Sam's strange and quite unfunny jokes. "No, my beloved has a very difficult past, and I don't want to give him any reason to doubt my feelings for him or his place here with me."

"What do you mean by a difficult past?" Dante asked, his features pinched up into a look of concern.

"I don't wish to disrespect my mate by telling his story without his permission, but as my friends, I know you would never hold judgement against him. I also wish for you to know so that you may help me welcome my mate into our group, while also helping me navigate our relationship the best I can."

"Of course we would never judge him," Ben insisted, reaching out to take my hand. "You are very important to us,

Bastian, and so is your mate. We're here to help both of you any way we can." Sam gave his best friend a proud smile while Dante melted into a puddle at his husband's feet.

"Thank you, Ben," I replied, squeezing his hand before releasing it. I told them everything I knew of Falcon's past, including the fake name he gave me and how frightened he was of his previous home. As I knew they would, they showed no signs of judgement, only concern as they listened.

"Shit," Sam muttered as I finished the story. His voice held no trace of its usual amusement.

"That's the saddest thing I've ever heard," Ben sniffled as tears streamed down his face.

"I'm so glad you found your beloved when you did," Dante added, pulling his weeping husband close to his side. "Fate's timing is always perfect."

"I'm not so sure about that; I wish I could have found him before he had to endure any of those terrible things. It kills me to know I can never take his pain away, but only make sure he never feels it again."

Sweet little Ben approached me and wrapped his arms around my waist, squeezing me as tightly as he could. A moment later, Dante joined in, followed by Sam. My friends held me, surrounding me with love and support, just as I knew they would do for Falcon.

"Thank you all," I whispered, barely keeping my emotions in check. My friends released me and gave me sad smiles.

"So, when *can* we meet Falcon?" Ben asked, breaking the silence.

"Well, tomorrow afternoon I'm escorting Dante downtown to-" Dante forcefully shook his head no, reminding me that the bookstore purchase was a surprise for his mate. "To take care of some business, but I was hoping you and Sam could keep him company while we're out. I would very much like for him to know he has friends here."

"As long as he's comfortable with it, I'd love that," Ben smiled. "Oh, I know! I'll make some cupcakes to welcome him!"

"Hell yeah," Sam smiled, rubbing his stomach. "Can you make strawberry?"

"They're for Falcon, not you," Ben insisted, propping his hand on his hip.

"Wait, I don't get any?"

"Well of course you do, but I want to be sure to make Falcon's favorite. Bastian, do you know what his favorite flavor is?"

"I don't," I answered sadly. "But I'll ask him in the morning and let you know." Ben nodded happily. "Dante, I was wondering if it would be okay for me to take the morning off tomorrow. My beloved is in need of clothing and a coat to make sure he's-"

"Of course it is," he replied, not even letting me finish my request. "Your mate's needs come first, always." I bowed my head in thanks.

"Aw, osito, you are the most wonderful man in the world," Ben gushed.

"It is not possible, for you hold that title, Amado." They kissed again, and again Sam rolled his eyes at the scene before him.

"I would like to ask a favor of you as well, Sam."

"What is it?"

"I would like for you to procure some condoms for me. I'm not sure what to shop for, and thought perhaps you would know which ones are best."

"I don't use that shit," he replied, scrunching up his nose. "And why are you?

We're impervious to disease, remember? That's a ticket to free love right there!"

"Because of my mate's past, he is uncomfortable partaking in any sexual activities without a condom, and I respect his wishes."

"Oh my god," Sam groaned. "He doesn't know you're a vampire, does he?" I shook my head no. "Are you gonna nearly croak like this guy?" he asked, thumbing over to Dante. "I swear, I don't understand why you all don't just come out with it. 'Hey there hot stuff, I'm a vampire, which means you'll live forever and we'll have lots of awesome sex for all eternity. Now let's go bang one out'. Who's gonna say no to that?"

Dante rubbed his temples while I shook my head at the ridiculous man. "I can only hope your mate is not human; I don't believe you have the tender care required to ease them into the situation."

Sam shrugged, not offended in the slightest. "Probably not." He sighed. "Okay, I'll get your condoms. I'll sneak them in while you two are out in the morning. Just be gentle when you use them with him; last time we fucked, you stretched my hole out so much, I nearly shit my pants the next day." Dante rubbed his forehead harder while Ben giggled behind his hand.

"See, that right there is the kind of thing I *don't* want you saying in front of Falcon."

"I'll try; honestly I will, but it's like asking a dog not to bark."

"Perhaps I should get you a shock collar," I teased.

Sam's jaw dropped. "Where was this kinky shit when we were fuck buddies?"

"Wait," Ben interrupted, looking confused. "You'd *want* to wear a collar?"

"Hell yeah," Sam answered, making his brows bounce again.

Ben turned to Dante. "Would you want *me* to wear a collar?" Ben had come out of his shell so much since he and Dante bonded; lately, anytime something sexual came up in conversation (which was often, considering he kept company with Sam), he blatantly asked Dante about his interest. He was becoming as insatiable as the rest of us. Well...perhaps maybe not Sam.

Dante's eyes darkened and the smell of his pheromones nearly knocked me over. "I want to do *everything* to you."

Ben let out a quiet moan. "Then let's go upstairs and get started." He giggled again when Dante scooped him up and tossed him over his shoulder. "Congratulations again, Bastian!" Ben called out as they exited my apartment. "Let me know tomorrow what kind of cupcakes to make!"

"Well, I guess I'll get back to my evening too," Sam said. "Don't want those two downstairs having all the fun without me." Just as he stepped through the doorway, he turned and gave me a kind smile. "I'm happy for you, man; really."

"Thank you, Sam."

He winked and shut the door behind him. I was too excited to sleep (not that I needed much; vampires only needed about two hours a night to be completely rested), so I sat outside Falcon's door, listening closely in case he needed anything.

Chapter Four

Milo

"You thought you could get away?" Jerome asked, shoving me in the same chair I'd sat in when he tattooed me. "I own you, remember? You belong to me."

"I...I belong with Bastian," I whispered, my body shaking as I watched Jerome dig a butcher's knife from the kitchen drawer.

"Shut the hell up!" he screamed and slapped me across the face. "You work for me and you will always belong to me. Hold him down, boys." Marcus and Andre laughed as they pinned me to the seat. "I think we need to show him what we do to traitors." Jerome grinned wickedly as he pressed the tip of the knife into my chest.

"No!" I swung my fists wildly, connecting with a hard surface. I couldn't believe it; I'd never struck Jerome before. I could only imagine what would happen to me now. I curled into the fetal position, trembling and waiting for the end to come. A light flicked on and a hand gently stroked my hair. "Stop messing with me!" I pleaded as tears began to fall. "Just kill me!"

"Cielito, it's okay," a warm voice crooned. "You're safe at home with me. You're having a nightmare. I'm here, Falcon. I'm right here." I blinked up to see Bastian standing over me, looking terrified and bleeding from the nose.

"Oh god!" I cried, sitting bolt upright. "I hit you! Oh Bastian, I'm so sorry! I didn't know what I was doing! I swear I'd never hurt you. Please don't send me back! Please!"

Bastian scooped me out of bed and held me tightly to his chest. "You are *never* going back there." I wept into his neck as he rocked me back and forth, kissing the entire surface of my head. "Estás a salvo en mis brazos, pequeño, y te tendré en mis brazos para siempre."

"I don't know what that means," I sniffled, "But it sounds beautiful."

Bastian chuckled softly and squeezed me tighter. "It means, 'You are safe in my arms, little one, and I will keep you in my arms forever'."

"Papi, that's all I want," I cried again. "I don't want to leave you. I want to stay with you forever. I'm so sorry I hit you. I didn't mean to."

"Shh, shh, it's okay," he soothed. "Look." He loosened his grip so I could look up to his face. The blood had already dried on his skin. He grabbed a tissue from the nightstand and blotted it away. "See? No harm done, Falcon." My heart clenched; both from gratitude toward Bastian for not only understanding what happened, but for comforting me when I was the one who hurt *him*, but also from guilt. Maybe since he didn't get upset when I punched him, he wouldn't get upset if he knew I'd been dishonest with him.

"It's Milo," I said quietly.

"I'm sorry?"

"My name. It's Milo; Milo Walker. Falcon is the name I've always given to men who asked for it. I'm so sorry I gave it to you. At first, I didn't know if I could trust you, but then I quickly found out I could but I felt too guilty to tell you the truth. I can't lie to you, Bastian. I care for you so much and I hope you're not mad at me, but I understand if you are."

"Oh, Milo," he whispered, pulling me close again. "I could never be mad at you, sweet man. Thank you so much for trusting me. You don't know what it means to me; what *you* mean to me." He kissed my temple and rocked me some more. I certainly wasn't an expert, but when he held me like this, it sure felt a lot like love; love from him toward me, and love blooming in my chest for him. Whatever it was, I didn't want to lose it.

"Will you stay with me tonight, Bastian?"

"Nothing would make me happier, Cielito."

He set me down on the bed and I scooted over to make room for his large body. Bastian climbed in behind me and wrapped a strong arm around my waist. The warmth of his body relaxed and soothed me as I snuggled back against him.

"Is this okay, Milo?"

I smiled; I loved the sound of my name on his lips. "It's perfect."

He kissed my cheek and pulled me even closer to him. "Yes it is."

*****

Bastian

I'd never been happier I needed such little sleep. Not only was I close when Milo needed me, but I got to spend most of the night relishing the feel of my beautiful mate in my arms. I would have happily skipped the couple of hours of sleep I got, but I didn't want to be tired during the day and miss out on anything Milo needed or wanted to do.

I felt the moment my beloved woke up. His breathing changed and he stretched slightly before touching his hands to my arm, which was still wrapped around his thin waist.

"You're still here," he whispered.

I flinched. "Would you like for me to leave?"

"No, no, no," he replied quickly. "It's just...this is so nice."

"It is," I agreed, pulling him even closer, though our bodies were already squished together. "Good morning, Milo." I loved saying his name; his *real* name, and loved the fact he told it to me even more. I'd won my mate's trust, and he'd even told me he cared for me greatly. Even better was that I could feel his love toward me, even if he hadn't said the words. I was sure my heart would burst if it tried to contain any more happiness.

"Good morning, Bastian." I hummed and sank my nose into his hair, taking deep breaths of his glorious scent. Milo chuckled. "Are you sniffing me?"

"Mm hmm," I answered, taking in another draw. "You smell so sweet. It's putting me in the mood for pancakes."

"Oh, I love pancakes. I haven't had them in so long."

"I can make you some if you're hungry."

"I'm starving!" After his declaration, Milo was surrounded by embarrassment and shame. I was sure he'd never been allowed to say such things before.

"Milo, remember what I told you; it makes me so happy to take care of you. I want to give you everything you need, so please don't be afraid to tell me those needs."

"Thank you, Papi," he replied quietly, stroking his fingers along the back of my hand.

"So, I'll go make us some breakfast and then we'll leave for the mall. How does that sound?"

"That sounds incredible."

"Good." I kissed his cheek and smiled when he hummed happily. "Your clothes were returned last night; I'll grab them from the living room."

"Would you mind if I take another shower before I get dressed?" Milo asked shyly.

"Of course not, Cielito. This is your home too; you're welcome to do whatever you wish. What's mine is yours."

He turned around to face me and wrapped me in a strong hug. "You are the most amazing man in the world."

"Not possible; you already hold that title." Okay, so I stole the line from Dante, but it was a good line! And I was happy I did it when Milo squeezed me even tighter before straining his neck up for a kiss. "Now, you enjoy your shower and I'll get to work on breakfast."

I gave Milo a new towel and his freshly laundered clothing before heading into the kitchen. I prepared a huge stack of pancakes and fried up a pound of bacon. Then, for good measure, I scrambled a dozen eggs. When Milo entered the kitchen after his shower, his eyes grew huge at the sight of all the food.

"Wow, what's the occasion?" he asked, excitedly surveying the platters.

"You're hungry," I answered simply. A strong wave of Milo's affection hit me, and I decided I would cook like this for him at every mealtime; not only just because it made him happy, which was reason enough, but because once we were bonded, he would inherit my increased metabolism, and I didn't want his health to suffer if he lost any more weight. Suddenly, Milo's nervousness mixed into the air. "Is something wrong, Cielito?"

"No, I was just thinking of something. I mean, I was wondering something." I cocked my head in confusion, and he continued, "I was wondering if you still wanted to be boyfriends."

"Of course I do," I answered quickly. "But...did I do something wrong as your sugar daddy?" If I did something my mate didn't like, I wanted to know so I could fix it immediately.

Milo shook his head. "No, you're amazing. It's just..." His lips squished up in thought. "This is hard to explain. Being a sugar daddy is about taking care of someone. Boyfriends take care of each *other*. And they care very much about each other. They are loyal and faithful to one another and try to make each other happy. Does that make sense?"

"Yes." Sort of. I was still a little unclear on human terms and rules for relationships, but I didn't care what Milo called us as long as he was happy and we were together. There was, however, one thing that concerned me. "If we're boyfriends, can you still call me Papi?"

Milo laughed and it was the most beautiful sound I'd ever heard. "Absolutely."

"Then yes," I nodded, making Milo laugh again. "I'm very glad we're boyfriends."

"Me too, Papi," Milo answered with a heart-stopping smile. "Me too."

*****

Milo

Bastian fed me so many pancakes I thought I would explode. As soon as I cleared my plate, he slapped another cake onto it and smothered it with butter and syrup. I'm not sure how many I ended up eating; I lost count after five. Plus, I gobbled up so much bacon, I was pretty sure I was more pig than man. And then there were the eggs on top of it all. One thing was certain; as long as Bastian kept me around, I'd never go hungry again.

After I was full to bursting, I waddled out to Bastian's SUV and he drove me to the mall. We talked and laughed the whole way, and I couldn't believe this was my life now. I had a boyfriend who took such wonderful care of me and made me happier than I ever dreamed of being.

The weather was warmer than it had been for the past several days, but there was still a nip in the air. Bastian insisted I wear his jacket in from the parking lot and I didn't fight him. Not only was I happy to have some of his clothing on me, I liked my body being covered up. Plus, it was one less layer he was wearing, which meant I got to enjoy the way his dark jeans melded to his thick thighs, and how his navy blue dress shirt hugged his trunk. Good lord, the man was gorgeous.

"Okay, Cielito; I think I know just the place," Bastian announced as we entered the shopping center. "May I hold your hand on the way?"

My heart skipped a beat. There was nothing more than I wanted than to lay claim to the man in public, but I wanted to double check with him first. "Are you sure? There are lots of people around."

Bastian leaned in closer to me and asked in a quiet voice, "Are you worried Jerome may be here to see you?"

"No, he'd never be in a place like this." This place was too happy and full of life for someone as evil as Jerome. "It's just...well, there may be people here who have seen me...you know...*working*. If you're not comfortable with them seeing us together, I understand."

Bastian flinched and rubbed his chest like I'd caused him physical pain. "Milo, I couldn't be more proud to have you on my arm," he insisted. "I will never push you, but

I would love to hold your hand and show everyone you're my boyfriend."

"I'd love it too." Bastian smiled and linked our fingers together and damn if he didn't look proud. He had a spring in his step as he led me through the mall and into a clothing store. He smiled widely and motioned his arm to dozens of racks full of trendy clothes of brightly colored fabric. My heart sank.

"Is something wrong?" he asked, looking concerned.

"No, these are nice if this is what you like." I reached for a hanger, but Bastian stopped me with a gentle touch to my arm.

"I want you to get what *you* like, Cielito. I only brought you here because these clothes resemble what you're wearing. If this is not your style, please tell me."

"You're being so nice to buy me new clothes, I didn't want you to be mad that I don't like these."

"Milo, I could never be mad at you. I don't think you realize how precious you are to me." He ran his fingers through my hair and tucked it behind my ear.

"I hate what I'm wearing," I admitted, looking down at my worn jeans and cropped shirt. "Jerome made me wear things like this because he said men liked tricks who looked more feminine."

"Oh, Cielito." Bastian took me in his arms. "I'm sorry; if I'd known, I never would have brought you here." And then he kissed me; slowly, deeply, and right there in front of everyone before resting his forehead on mine. "Please lead me to any store you like. I want you to get what makes you happy."

"Thank you, Papi." *I love you,* I wanted to say, but I was nervous. I'd only been with him for a short time; I wasn't sure how long I was supposed to wait to say such things. Instead, I hugged him tightly and hoped he could feel what I was too afraid to say.

I led him into a store that made my pulse race as I looked around at all the clothing; all the black, leather, spiked, ripped clothing. I chewed on my lip and slowly panned over to look at Bastian to see how he was handling everything. A slow smile crossed his lips as he took in the sights, his head bobbing to the heavy metal that blasted over the store's speakers. "I like it."

I slammed my body into his and reached up to grab the back of his head. When he bent over so I could reach him, I peppered his face with kisses as he laughed. The raspy, booming sound gave me goosebumps.

"Will you try some things on for me?"

"Really?"

Bastian nodded and then laughed again when I zoomed around the store, collecting anything that captured my interest, which was basically everything. He requested a fashion show, so I led him to a hallway of dressing rooms in the back where he sat in a chair to wait. I went into a room and sighed happily as I looked over the pieces I brought in.

I pulled on a pair of black skinny jeans that were ripped to hell and a black long sleeved shirt which also had holes on the shoulders. My pulse quickened as I examined myself in the mirror. Maybe it was silly to be getting so worked up over clothes, but they meant so much to me; they were a choice *I* got to make on how to express myself. The dark colors and edgy rips and patterns made me feel masculine, tough, and in control.

I took a deep breath and pushed the changing room door open. I stepped out into the hallway, nervous to find out what

Bastian thought. When he spotted me, however, his face lit up with a toothy grin and he stood to meet me.

"You look stunning."

"Really?" I asked, my own smile now taking over.

"Absolutely." He cupped my cheek with his large hand. "And you know what my favorite part is?" Bastian trailed his thumb across my bottom lip. "This smile."

I didn't know what to say; how to convey how happy I was - how happy *he'd* made me, so I wrapped my arms around his waist and squeezed tightly. I nuzzled my head into his chest and sighed as he squeezed me back just as tight.

"May I see more?" he asked after a few minutes of snuggling. I nodded quickly and released him to jog back to my dressing room.

Each time I stepped out wearing a new outfit, Bastian gushed over it and complimented me until I could barely carry my head with how big it'd swelled from my inflated ego. I'd never had much (if any) self confidence, but Bastian made me feel like the most handsome man on earth.

"This is the last one," I announced when I emerged wearing yet another pair of black jeans (though these weren't ripped) and a gray sweater that covered my fingers and had holes for my thumbs to poke through.

"Gorgeous," Bastian smiled. "Though I think something's missing." I looked down at my outfit in confusion until I saw him grab a box from beneath his seat. "I found these while you were getting dressed. What do you think?" He opened the lid to reveal a pair of tall black combat boots, decked out with buckles and chains which were crossed over the laces. Luckily, there was a zipper up the back of each shoe so I wouldn't have to fasten everything.

"I think they're amazing," I whispered. Bastian looked so proud that he'd picked something out that I liked. He dropped to his knees before me, rolled a long black sock up over each of my feet, and helped me into the boots. "They feel amazing too."

"Then you shall have them," he insisted when he stood back up. "There's just one more thing…" He reached into his pocket and pulled out a thick black leather bracelet. It had a braid around the center and long straps on each end as a closure. *I must have taken longer than I thought admiring myself in the mirror,* I thought, assuming Bastian had found the bracelet in the store as well and already paid for it.

"This bracelet has been in my family for centuries," he explained. "It is crafted from Spanish leather. I would like for you to wear it, Cielito."

"Bastian, it's beautiful," I whispered, running my fingers along the supple leather. "Are you sure you want me to have it?"

"I'm positive, Milo." He fished my thumb out of my sweater and pushed my sleeve up my forearm, revealing the tattoo Jerome had carved into my skin. "I hope you know I love every inch of your skin, even this patch that is marred by the terrible actions of a terrible man." He lifted my wrist to his lips and tenderly kissed the scar. "But I know how you feel about it, and what it represents to you. I ask that you wear this bracelet over the scar as a reminder of your new life and that I am always with you."

Bastian placed the cuff around my wrist and tied the leather strips in a pretty bow. "If you ever decide you'd like a new tattoo to cover this one, or to have this horrible lie removed from your skin, I will happily provide you with that, but only if you wish."

"Thank you, Bastian," I whispered as a tear trailed down my cheek. He bent down and kissed it away. "I don't know how to thank you for this; for everything."

"Your happiness is all the thanks I need." He kissed my lips tenderly and stood tall, looking prouder and happier than I'd ever seen him.

"I wish I didn't have to put my other clothes back on," I thought out loud.

"You don't," he shrugged before popping the tags off of the clothes I was wearing and gathering everything else out of the dressing room. "I shall pay for these new ones and you can wear them out."

"Thank you," I repeated, unsure what else to say.

Bastian nodded and carried everything up to the register, where a man around my age rang him up. The man's stoic face was covered in piercings and he had shaggy black hair that covered one eye.

"These tags belong to the outfit my boyfriend is currently wearing," Bastian announced as he handed them across the counter. He looked so pleased to be telling the seemingly uninterested man that I was his boyfriend. "He would like to wear it when we leave."

The cashier looked me over and jutted his chin at me. "You look sick, dude."

Bastian gasped and turned on me, looking me up and down before placing the back of his hand on my forehead. "*Are* you sick, Cielito? Did you get too tired from trying on clothes? Are you hungry?"

I erupted into laughter and even the cashier's pierced lip twitched into a little smile. "No, Papi, I'm fine. It's slang; sick means good."

"Oh." Bastian sighed with relief and smiled widely at me. "Then you look positively under the weather."

The cashier snorted a laugh and I chuckled again, wrapping my sweet, silly man in a big hug. "Thanks, Papi."

The total of my clothes came up to over twelve hundred dollars. I tried to convince Bastian I didn't need that much, but he just waved me off and happily swiped his credit card, telling me I deserved all of it and so much more. When my boyfriend wasn't looking, the cashier gave me a thumbs up, and I smiled with a nod. I knew how lucky I was.

When we stepped into the hall, I jogged over to a trash can and threw away my old jeans, crop top and dilapidated sneakers. I flipped them off for good measure, making Bastian laugh. He carried all of the bags of my new clothes in one hand (which made me deliriously proud; my man was so strong) and held my hand in his other. He took me to a few more stores, buying me a ton of socks, underwear, and a puffy black coat. I was downright spoiled.

"Are you hungry for lunch, Milo? We've got time to eat before I have to go downtown with Dante."

"I'm still pretty full from breakfast."

"Are you sure? I know a place that makes a great cheeseburger."

Mm, cheeseburger. My stomach gave a growl just thinking about a burger and fries. "I guess I'm hungrier than I thought." Bastian squeezed my hand and smiled as he led me back out to the parking lot.

Chapter Five

Jerome

"We found him," Marcus said as he and Andre came into the house. They sat down at the table next to me where I was cleaning my gun.

"Where?" I barked, not taking my eyes from my work.

"Across town," Andre replied. "We went for a pick up and saw him leaving a burger joint."

"He was dressed like a fucking emo," Marcus said, and they both laughed. "As if we wouldn't recognize his scrawny ass."

"Am I laughing?" I growled, slamming my gun down on the table. Both men flinched as their dumb grins disappeared. "That little whore has dirt on us. We can't have him running free." Granted, I had an inside man at the local precinct, but if he went to the Feds, we were fucked. I picked up my pistol, loaded it, and pointed it at Marcus's head with narrowed eyes. "You have three seconds to explain why you didn't bring him back here with you."

"He wasn't alone," Marcus replied quickly.

Andre fished his phone from his pocket, tapped the screen, and turned it toward me. "He was with this man." I examined the photo of an intimidating figure.

"Who the fuck is that?"

"We think he works for Javier Corp," Marcus offered. "We followed them to their headquarters when they left the restaurant. We're assuming he's in security."

"Fuck." We didn't need Javier Corp on our asses. They controlled half the fucking city; if that little faggot ratted us out, we'd be in serious shit. I dropped my weapon and Marcus sighed with relief. "Tail him but don't let him see you. The second he's away from his bodyguard, grab him. Rough him up if you want, but when you deliver him to me, I want him alive and conscious. I want to see the fear in his eyes when I kill him."

Both men's mouths curled up into evil grins. "You got it."

Chapter Six

Milo

I chewed on my fingernails as I waited for Bastian's friends to arrive. I was nervous to meet them, and even more nervous to spend time with them without my boyfriend here as a buffer. Bastian asked over lunch if I was interested in hanging out with Sam and Ben while he left for town, and I agreed. I really did want to meet them because I knew it was important to Bastian, and if I were honest, I'd like to have some friends of my own, but now I was growing more anxious by the second.

"Are you sure you're okay with this, Cielito?" Bastian asked, sitting down beside me on the couch. He had changed into a black suit and tie for his business with Dante, and he looked breathtakingly gorgeous; he was handsome in anything he wore, but his suit gave him an intimidating, professional edge. He wrapped his arm around my shoulders and I lay my head on his chest. "I can cancel with them if you'd prefer."

"No, I don't want to seem rude."

"They will understand, I assure you."

"I want to meet them," I said with more confidence than I felt, and Bastian kissed my temple. "I'm just a little worried." Especially when it came to Sam. I didn't mean to judge him before I met him, but I wasn't sure what to expect from a bodyguard. Bastian was huge and strong but treated me with a gentle touch; could Sam be the same?

"There's nothing to be worried about," he soothed, caressing his hand up and down my arm. "They'll love you; I'm sure of it. And I really think you'll enjoy their company as well. Ben is sweet as pie and Sam...well,

Sam is more of an *acquired* taste, but he is a good man."

Before either of us could say more, a knock sounded on Bastian's front door. He helped me from the couch and held my hand as we walked through the living room to the entrance to the apartment; I was sure he could feel my fingers trembling in his. Before he opened the door, Bastian leaned down to kiss my cheek and gave me a gentle smile. "I'm right here with you, Cielito. If you decide you're not ready for this, just tell me. I promise no one will be upset." I swallowed hard and nodded my head.

When Bastian opened the door, I was greeted by the sight of a small man with big, pretty blue eyes who stood a couple of inches shorter than me. I assumed him to be Ben. He and the much larger man by his side were both smiling widely. I would have guessed the other man to be Ben's bodyguard based on his stature, but the fact that they were holding hands made me think this was his husband.

"Dante, Ben, I would like you to meet my boyfriend Milo," Bastian announced, grinning as brightly as the other two men. Ben's face shone even more at the sound of my name, but Dante was the first to speak.

"It's a pleasure," he greeted, holding out his hand. I took it with mine and shook politely.

"Oh Milo, it's so nice to meet you!" Ben gushed before I could even answer his husband. He waved Dante's hand away from mine so that he could take it, while Dante just chuckled. "I've been driving osito crazy all day with how excited I've been. I made you cupcakes!" He held up a basket in his free hand, which I hadn't even noticed him holding. "They're chocolate; Bastian told me earlier that they were your favorite."

"They are," I answered with a smile; it was impossible not to immediately like the little sweetheart in front of me; the man made me cupcakes for goodness sake! "Thank you."

"You're welcome." He leaned in closer to me to whisper, "I made extra since Sam will be here with us. He eats a *lot*!"

"I heard that!" sounded from the elevator behind Ben. I assumed the voice belonged to Sam, though I couldn't see him yet.

Ben giggled and Dante looked down at his husband with a goofy, lovesick expression that made me smile. "Milo, I *love* your sweater," Ben added, running his fingers down the soft fabric on my arm. "See, Sam? I'm not the only person my age who wears sweaters!"

Sam stepped in from behind Ben and I was shocked; he was only about an inch taller than me, and though he was a little thicker, he wasn't mega-muscular like I was expecting. He looked like an average, cute guy; not at all what I assumed out of a bodyguard.

Sam looked back and forth between my shirt and Ben's, which was long and brown, and worn overtop a pair of pressed khakis. "Babe, do you seriously not see a difference between the two?" *Babe*? I looked to Bastian in confusion, but he didn't seem surprised at the endearment. Dante looked a little perturbed, though.

"Well, his *is* a little shorter," Ben said, cocking his head to the side as he inspected my shirt again.

Sam chuckled. "God, you're adorable. Which, by the way, is why *you* should wear shorter sweaters too. How many times do I have to beg you to show off that juicy ass?" *Okay, now I'm seriously confused.* "Take a lesson from Bastian's man here; he's in a comfy sweater but still showing what his mama gave him. You should too!"

"I'd appreciate it if you kept your eyes off of my man," Bastian growled, sending a thrill through me.

"You guys are so greedy," Sam pouted. "Granted, you saw Milo's ass first, but I saw Ben's first, so I should still get viewing rights. Besides, I hold the record for three bounces when I spank it."

Dante gritted his teeth and clenched his fists, looking like he wanted to choke the life out of Sam, but Ben just giggled. "Actually, Dante broke your record last night! He got it to bounce four times! Of course, I was naked though; I think that made a big difference."

"*What?* God dammit, Dante! I've held that record for nearly a year! Come here and take your pants off, babe; I need to get my title back."

"Touch my husband and you'll lose your hand," Dante threatened. I didn't doubt his words, but they didn't seem to affect Sam.

"So greedy," he repeated before turning to me. "Don't you think?"

I blinked at him before looking to Bastian for help. "Ignore him, Cielito; it's the only way to shut him up." Sam's jaw dropped in offense, but my attention was drawn to Ben's gasp. His hand was cradled over his heart.

"You call him Cielito? Little heaven? That's so sweet! It's just like the beautiful Spanish nickname my Dante gave me." Dante smiled and leaned down to give his husband a kiss.

Sam groaned. "Spoiler alert; they're gross like this all the time."

"We're not *gross*," Dante insisted after peeling his lips from Ben. "We're in love."

"Don't you have somewhere else to be?" Sam asked with an eye roll.

"Unfortunately yes," Bastian answered before taking me by the hand and leading me a few feet away. "What do you think, Milo?" he whispered. "Are you comfortable staying here with Ben and Sam?"

"I'm a little confused, but not uncomfortable," I whispered back, making Bastian chuckle. "I think it might be fun to spend some time with them."

"Thank you, Cielito." He pecked my lips and wrapped me in a hug. "Call me if you need anything and I'll hurry home. I shall miss you, Milo."

My heart swelled in my chest. "I'll miss you too."

"Okay, okay," Sam interrupted, pulling me away from Bastian. "I can't handle two gross couples at once. Bastian, we will take good care of him. Now get the fuck out of here so we can have some fun."

Bastian gave Sam a long, unimpressed look before waving goodbye to me and walking to the door. He waited patiently for Dante to finish up his makeout session with his husband, and then the two of them disappeared into the hallway.

"Thank god, I thought they'd never leave," Sam groaned. He grabbed Ben's hand and dragged him over to the couch, took his basket of cupcakes to set on the coffee table, and pulled his friend down next to him, snuggling him close. "I hardly ever get to cuddle you anymore, let alone grope you." I didn't quite know what to think of the duo.

"Come sit with us, Milo," Ben requested, patting the sofa cushion beside him while he smiled sweetly. I sat down on the couch but left a large gap between us. I wanted to spend time with them, but wasn't comfortable being part of the cuddle party. "We want to hear all about you."

My anxiety spiked. I was hoping to avoid talking about myself and especially my history as much as possible since I had no idea how the two of them would react. I really did want friends, and I was worried if they knew about my past they may not be as accepting as they seemed to be so far.

"Oh, um..." I turned my gaze to my legs and picked at invisible lint on my pants. "Has Bastian not mentioned anything about me?" I wasn't sure what to hope for; I understood if he wasn't keen on telling his friends his boyfriend was a prostitute, but I also wished I didn't have to hash everything out on my own. I *definitely* wished Bastian was with me now.

"He did," Ben hedged while Sam gave me a sad smile, "But I meant we wanted to hear about what you like to do for fun or what makes you happy; just get to know you."

"Oh." I relaxed until I realized what he said. "Wait, Bastian told you about my past?" Ben's sad smile now matched Sam's as they both nodded. "And you still want to be here with me?"

"Of course we do!" Ben reached over and stopped my fake lint-picking to take my hand. "Milo, I hate what you've been through, but we would never judge you for it! The only person who should feel bad about it is Jerome, but that would require him to have a soul."

"Listen, Milo, I've had sex with a lot of guys," Sam interjected. "Like...a *lot*. I mean, a crazy amount of dicks have been-"

"Sam," Ben interrupted his friend.

"Right, sorry. Anyway, my point is this; everybody who lives here knows that, but nobody judges me for it. People don't avoid me because they think I'm dirty or something like that; if they avoid me, it's because I get on their nerves." Ben nodded his agreement and I tried very hard not to smile. "But I was with all of those guys because I *chose* to be. You didn't get that choice, Milo. Jerome took it away from you and we all hate him for it. If I ever meet that guy, I'll happily remove his balls from his body," he finished, and damn if he didn't look serious.

Ben smiled at his friend before turning it on me. "I'm not strong enough to remove body parts, but I feel the same way. So does Dante and of course Bastian does too. He didn't tell us about your past because he wanted to warn us or give us the option to stay away or anything like that. He told us because he knew we care. He cares about you too; he told us how strong and brave you are, and that he's so incredibly proud of you. He loves you, Milo." I gasped and felt my eyes grow wide. "Has he not told you yet?" I shook my head no. "Well, he does. You can tell by the way he looks at you."

"But…we've only been together a couple of days."

"So?" Ben shrugged. "My Dante said he fell in love with me the second he saw me for the first time. It's how things work with v…um…virile Spanish men. They're very romantic."

Sam snorted. "Nice save, babe." Ben gave his friend a look of annoyance. I had no idea what was going on between them, but also didn't care; I was too focused on Ben's assertion. *Bastian loves me.*

"Can we please eat cupcakes now?" Sam asked, sticking his bottom lip out and rounding his eyes.

"You know I can't resist that puppy face," Ben said before grabbing the basket of goodies off of the coffee table. He gave Sam a cake before handing one to me. I removed my thumbs from my sleeves and pushed the fabric up so I didn't get frosting on my shirt. "Ooh, I love that bracelet."

"Thank you. Bastian gave it to me." I ran my fingers along the supple leather and decided to go for broke. If we were all friends now, they'd see it sooner or later. I took a deep breath and untied the straps. "It's to cover this."

"Oh, Milo," Ben gasped. Tears clouded his eyes as he brushed his finger along the tattoo. "I'm so sorry."

"Bastian said it doesn't bother him," I explained quickly, wanting to defend my boyfriend. "It's not that he's trying to cover it up so he doesn't have to look at it or something. He says he loves my skin; he just knows I hate this and what it stands for."

Ben nodded and smiled gently. "I know. Dante feels the same way about my scars." He sat his treat on the table and pushed up his own sleeves, revealing several pink lines over the insides of his wrists. "He says they'll always be beautiful to him because they mean I survived and am still with him."

"Did you cut yourself?" I asked, then immediately flinched at how intrusive the question was.

"No," Ben answered, smiling slightly to let me know I hadn't offended him. "I was kidnapped last month by someone who was jealous of Dante's wealth and power."

"The sick fuck tortured him and tried to kill him," Sam growled. He was intimidating even with chocolate frosting in his teeth.

"Holy shit. How did you escape?"

"I was rescued. Dante, Sam and Bastian saved me." He took my hand once more. "Your boyfriend is a good man; strong, brave and loyal."

"Thank you," I whispered, full to the brim with pride for my amazing man. The three of us ate our snacks in silent thought.

When we were finished, Ben wiped his mouth and turned to me again.

"So, on to happier things. What do you like to do for fun?"

"Um...I like to eat," I offered lamely.

"You're in luck," Sam smiled and pointed his thumb to Ben. "This guy is the best fucking cook there is."

"Bastian said you were a master in the kitchen," I told the small man.

"Aw, he did?" Ben asked with a wide smile. "I'm going to save him a cupcake." I suddenly felt guilty for ever having negative thoughts about the sweet man.

"Do you think you could show me some cooking tips sometime?" I asked nervously. I hated being so forward and quickly explained, "I never learned how and I'd love to be able to make something for Bastian."

"That sounds so fun!" Ben squealed. "I've offered to teach Sam, but he only wants to eat what *I* cook."

"Can you blame me?" he asked before shoving another cupcake in his mouth.

Ben giggled before saying, "I'd love to teach you some stuff, Milo. So, besides eating, what else do you like to do?"

"I like to...shower." *My god, can I get any more pathetic?* It wasn't like my previous life left me much room for hobbies, though.

"Oh, Dante and I have a big waterfall shower in our relaxation room I bet you'd love," Ben smiled. "You're welcome to use it whenever you like."

"Really?" I couldn't believe he was not only *not* making fun of me for being so boring, he was offering his home to me after knowing me a total of twenty minutes.

"Of course! We also have a jacuzzi tub that Sam and I like to hang out in together. With our underwear on!" he added quickly, making me and Sam laugh. "The three of us should have a jacuzzi party one day!"

"That sounds amazing," I smiled. "Oh hey, I bet Bastian's home theater is your relaxation room." Sam and Ben both gave me confused looks. "I mean, Bastian doesn't have a jacuzzi room, but he has a big theater. Come check it out!" I led them into the room with the huge screen and comfy furniture. "I almost forgot about it because we haven't used it together yet. I love movies; Bastian has some really good scary ones." Sam helped himself, walking over to the DVD cabinet and rifling through it.

"Do you see any vampire movies in there?" Ben asked his friend.

Sam snorted. "Ben looooves vampires."

The little sweetie nodded at me. "They're such misunderstood creatures. Everyone thinks they're so scary and mean, but they can be romantic and wonderful. And did you know garlic doesn't really make them sick?"

I blinked at him. "Are you saying you think vampires are real?"

"Of course they are. In fact, they might be closer than you think." He flicked his eyebrows at me while smiling widely. *Okay, the sweetie has a weird streak. I love it.*

"I'm not in the mood for a vampire movie," Sam argued, still digging through the cabinet. "I'm looking for porn."

"Sam!" Ben scolded, instantly blushing.

"What? Look how big that screen is! If Bastian doesn't watch porn on that thing, that's just a waste of resources. Wait, is it a 3D screen?" he asked excitedly.

"I don't think so," I answered quietly. My gut was tied up in knots over the possibility of Bastian having naughty movies in his collection. I know it was hypocritical, due to my history and how accepting Bastian had been of it, but the thought of him getting pleasure from other men - even the sight of them, made me uncomfortable.

"Holy shit, look what I found!" Sam exclaimed.

"Is...is it porn?" I asked, my stomach dropping even further. Ben must have sensed my unease, because he grabbed up both of my hands and shook his head.

"Even if it is, trust me; Bastian will have no desire for it now that he has you. I promise." I decided Ben was the sweetest man on earth. Well, second only to my Bastian.

"Unfortunately, I can't find any of that," Sam pouted and I breathed a sigh of relief. "But I found something almost as good. Check it out!" He pulled several movie cases from the back of the cabinet. "Chick flicks! Oh my god, I can't wait to give Bastian so much shit over these."

I propped my hands on my hips. "You better not do that...without letting me be there to watch." It was so funny that my big brute enjoyed mushy movies, and a little good-natured teasing wouldn't hurt.

Sam tipped his head back and laughed. "Oh, I like you."

"I think it's sweet he has these," Ben countered, taking the films and looking them over.

"You would," Sam said with an eye roll, and I covered my mouth to keep from laughing. "Here we go; I found the perfect movie." He held up a DVD, whose cover had a picture of a man holding a chainsaw.

"Nice," I nodded.

"A slasher film?" Ben murmured, all the color draining from his face. "I don't know if I can. There will be so much blood."

"It's fake, babe," Sam soothed. "And I'll hold your hand the whole time."

"Okay, I'll try."

Throughout the movie, Sam and I laughed at how stupid the characters were as they hid in obvious spots or made way too much noise when trying to evade the killer, and Ben hid his face in Sam's shoulder during any gory scenes; which there were a lot of. Given what I'd been through, these types of movies should bother me, but I loved them. Maybe it was because I knew it was all fake, or maybe it was because I liked seeing the good guys get away at the end. Maybe it was because I'd lived through something much scarier than this.

"Okay, I need something happy after that," Ben insisted when the movie ended. "Where are those chick flicks?"

"I've got a better idea," Sam said with a wicked smile. "Milo, I think it's time to officially initiate you into our weird little group."

"Initiate me?" Fear rose inside me, but I tamped it down, reminding myself these men were my friends and wouldn't do anything to hurt me.

"Yep. Doing stupid shit is kind of a requirement to hang out with us," he added, and Ben grinned widely while nodding his agreement. "We love to do stupid bets with even stupider stakes."

"Nothing too crazy, and never dangerous," Ben added. "Just fun stuff."

"You in?" Sam asked, giving me a hopeful expression.

Knowing Ben enjoyed the game, along with his assurance nothing bad would happen, I was excited to do something with them that concreted me into their group. "I'm in."

"Yay!" Ben clapped. "Wait a minute...what are we going to bet on?"

Sam swished his lips in thought before his face lit up. "I know!" He dug a quarter out of his pocket. "We'll bet on this." He looked to us for approval, and we both shrugged and nodded. At least a coin flip was simple to understand. "Okay babe, you and I will start out." He steadied the quarter on his thumbnail and flipped it into the air. "Call it!"

"Heads!" Ben exclaimed.

Sam caught the coin and slapped it onto the back of his wrist. When he peeked under his hand, his mouth curled up into a sneaky grin. "Well, well, looky here." He showed the coin to Ben, whose shoulders slumped.

"Dang it." He sighed. "I suppose you brought the lipstick?"

"Of course I brought the fucking lipstick," Sam assured as he dug it from his pocket. I guessed they played this game often. "And your forehead is looking a little bare. Lean in here." Ben did as he asked and Sam went to work. I watched and chuckled as he carefully and methodically drew an impressive penis over Ben's entire forehead.

"You're drawing a dick, aren't you?" Ben sighed.

"Do you even have to ask, babe?" He finished his work and recapped the lipstick. "Although, I think I did *too* good a job; looking at it is making me horny."

I burst into laughter. "You're not serious."

"Like hell I'm not! Look at that detail! Not to mention all those sexy red pubes. God, I love redheads."

I shook my head in amusement and disbelief, while Ben didn't seem to find Sam's words odd in the slightest. He simply retrieved his phone from his pocket and used its camera to inspect his friend's work.

"Ooh, I like the vein you put on there. That *is* good detail!" I laughed again and scrubbed a hand over my face. I couldn't believe I was worried about hanging out with these two; I was having an awesome time. "Okay, Milo; how about you and me?"

"Sure," I smiled.

Sam once again flipped the coin. "Call it, Milo!"

"Tails!"

He slapped the coin over and peeked. "Uh oh; sorry dude." He held his arm out to me to see the heads-up coin. I looked to Ben for my task.

The little man tapped his chin in thought before breaking out into giggles. "I've got it! You have to call Bastian and tell him you've decided to get your nipples pierced." He erupted into giggles again. The prank was cute, but the way he was cracking himself up was what really got me.

"Okay, I'll do it." The pair smiled at me and nodded in encouragement. "Oh, um...I don't have a phone. Sorry."

"Don't apologize," Ben insisted. "Here, you can use mine." He typed in a phone number and held it out to me.

"Bastian hasn't bought you a phone yet?" Sam asked, looking irritated. "While you've got him on the line, let me ask him what the fuck his problem is."

"Please don't," I begged. "It's no big deal. I don't have anyone to call anyway."

"You have us," Ben corrected with a smile, and Sam nodded.

My heart swelled and a huge grin crossed my face. "Thanks, guys." Sam winked at me and Ben patted my knee. "Here goes." I pressed the green phone icon and listened as the line rang. Ben reached over and placed the call on speakerphone.

"Ben?" Bastian's deep voice answered, sounding concerned.

"No, Papi, it's me." At hearing my pet name for Bastian, Ben gasped and covered his heart. Sam snorted and rolled his eyes at his dramatic friend.

"Is something wrong? Dante and I are on our way back, I'll be home soon and-"

"No, no, nothing's wrong," I replied quickly. "It's just...well, I was talking with Ben and Sam and I've decided something."

"What is it, Cielito?"

"I've decided I want to get my nipples pierced." Ben laughed out loud and Sam slapped his hand over his friend's mouth. He was grinning widely himself.

"Oh, Milo," Bastian answered in a husky voice. "That is so incredibly sexy." Ben's eyes widened and his chest shook with silent laughter. Sam just nodded slowly while still grinning ear to ear. "I love watching you react when I play with your nipples. I can only imagine how erotic it will be for both of us once they are pierced and tender. Everything will be more sensitive, and I wonder if I could get you to orgasm just by licking them." Suddenly, Ben wasn't laughing anymore. His eyes were huge and his mouth hung open (Sam had dropped his hand and was also staring at me wide-eyed).

I swallowed thickly. "O...okay, Papi, that um...that sounds amazing. I'll see you soon."

"Farewell, Cielito." The line went dead.

"Well that was certainly unexpected," Ben said after a moment of collecting himself.

"It didn't do anything to cure my horniness, that's for sure," Sam added. I snorted a laugh, not offended in the slightest; I figured a strong breeze would give Sam a stiffy.

"I think I'll be getting my nipples pierced for real," I announced, and my friends finally snapped out of their stupor to laugh.

"Wow, I'm not sure how we'll follow that, but it looks like it's you and me, Milo,"

Sam said, repositioning the coin on his thumb. "Your call."

"Heads."

He flipped the quarter and held his arm out for me to inspect. "It's heads. Hit me with your best shot."

I thought hard about something good enough to impress the two guys who were experts at this. "Okay, keeping on the nipple theme, you have to take a picture of yours and let me send it to any person in your phone I choose."

"That's incredible!" Ben giggled. "Great job, Milo!" I puffed up with pride at his compliment, even if it *was* over something silly.

"Yeah, good work," Sam agreed, "But I've got to warn you; most people in my phone have already seen it." I had no doubt, but it was the best I could come up with. Sam slipped his hand under his shirt.

"What are you doing?" Ben asked curiously.

"I'm getting it hard. If this picture turns out good enough, it might score me a lay tonight." He licked his thumb and put it to his skin before lifting his shirt, positioning his phone's camera and looking at the reflection of his glistening peak. "Perfect." The shutter sounded and he passed his phone to me. "Here, I've got my contacts pulled up; you just have to choose a name and hit send."

I scrolled through an endless list of men's names before a bolt of inspiration hit me. "What's your mom's name?"

Sam barked out a laugh, but it was Ben who answered, "Lucy! Her name is Lucy! Oh, do it, Milo!"

Turns out I didn't need to ask, though, as I saw 'Mom' listed in his contacts when I continued scrolling. Of course it made sense, but I wasn't expecting it at first because I always had to call my father by his first name. "And...send."

Ben broke into giggles again and Sam gave me a proud smile. "That was awesome. I knew I liked you." I beamed at his praise, and a moment later, Sam's phone pinged. He looked at the message and laughed out loud. "She asked why I sent her a picture of a weird mushroom."

I joined him in his laughter, and poor Ben lost his mind. The little sweetie rolled around on the floor, yelling that he was going to pee his pants, which only made Sam and me laugh harder. This was amazing; I was hanging out with guys my age, acting like morons together in my boyfriend's theater in his fancy house. Life couldn't get any better.

Suddenly, the door to the theater opened and in came Bastian and Dante, wearing matching huge grins.

"It sounds like you three had a great time," Dante said, warmly watching his lover roll around on the floor.

"We had the *best* time!" Ben corrected. He rose to his feet and ran to Dante, jumping into his arms when he got close.

Dante chuckled when he saw the artwork on Ben's forehead. "Oh Benny, what am I going to do with you?"

"Keep me and love me forever?"

"My thoughts exactly," Dante replied before giving him a kiss. Sam was right; they *were* a little gross, but in an absolutely adorable way.

"I missed you, osito. Are you okay?" Ben rubbed his hand in a circle over his husband's chest, as if he was trying to soothe away the pain of being apart.

"I'm better now."

Ben giggled and turned to my boyfriend. "How are you, Bastian?" he asked, placing a hand to his chest. I wasn't jealous. I could see Ben was head over heels for his husband, and that he cared for Bastian the way he cared for Sam; as a good friend.

"I'm okay," Bastian answered, patting Ben's hand before he pulled it away. "But I'm very glad to be back home to Milo." His eyes met mine and the warmth and affection they held for me melted me to the spot.

"Good god, I'm not gonna survive this mush fest," Sam pouted, but we all ignored him.

"Benny, I have a surprise for you," Dante said with a smile. "I was going to wait to give it to you, but I'm afraid I am just too excited." He pulled a folded paper from his suit jacket pocket and handed it to Ben, who narrowed his eyes as he looked it over. "It's the deed to *Page Turners*, or whatever you choose to name it now. It is yours, Amorcito."

"You bought me a *bookstore*?" Ben asked, his large eyes stretched even wider. "Oh, Tay, thank you!" Tears spilled down his face as he tackled his husband in a tight hug. "You are so wonderful and I love you so much!"

"I love you too, Benny. Come; let us go celebrate." Dante scooped his lover into his arms and left the room as Ben covered his neck in kisses, leaving no doubt as to what their 'celebration' would be. I wondered if they'd even take the time to scrub the dick off of Ben's face.

"Guess I'll get out of your hair too," Sam offered. "I think I'll head down to the club to look for my *own* celebration. Thanks for hanging out today, Milo. It was fun."

"Yes it was. Thanks, Sam. Maybe the five of us could get together some time?"

"Sounds great. Later, guys." He waved and left Bastian and me alone in the theater.

"It makes me so happy that you enjoyed yourself, Cielito," Bastian grinned. He crossed the room and pulled me from the couch onto my feet. His fingers combed through my hair before tucking it behind my ears; it was a simple gesture he'd done so many times, but always made me smile. The large man's tender touches were just for me. "But I did miss you terribly."

"I missed you too, Papi." I placed my palms on his stomach, enjoying the firmness of his body even through the layers of his suit. Being in his arms was like nothing I'd ever experienced; his touch made me feel warm, protected and...loved. Ben's words from earlier danced around my head. I felt the emotion from Bastian, but I was greedy and wanted to hear it as well. "Bastian, do you love me?" I blurted out. It wasn't exactly how I intended to ask him, but it was out there now and I couldn't take it back.

"I do," he answered easily, a gentle smile tugging on his lips. "Very much."

My heart pounded at how readily he answered, and how there was absolutely no doubt or hesitation in his voice. "I love you too." I barely got the last word out before Bastian took my lips in a long, slow kiss as he pressed our bodies together. "I was afraid to say it so soon," I explained once he released me. "I was afraid you'd think I was crazy or something, but Ben said he could tell you loved me. And I love you too. I love this house and this life you've given me, the friends you've shown me, just...everything, Bastian."

"You make my heart soar, Cielito," he replied, bending to rest his forehead to mine. "I dreamed of the day my soulmate would come into my life, but I never imagined it could be this incredible. You are the blood in my veins and the breath in my lungs. I cannot survive without you, Milo. You have all of the love in my heart for all time."

His sweet words made my knees weak. I gripped his waist for support and Bastian pressed his lips to mine. We took our time nibbling and tasting each other, and then I slowly sank my tongue into his mouth. He moaned as our flavors mingled and our slick flesh glided against one another. I explored every inch of his delicious mouth before pulling back to look into his heavy-lidded eyes.

"Bastian, I want you." I was hard as steel and could feel his answering firm cock pressing into my stomach. "I *need* you." I craved his beautiful body so strongly it actually hurt.

Bastian lifted me into his arms and carried me into his bedroom without taking his gaze off of mine. I saw my own need reflecting in his blown pupils. He lay me gently on his bed and kissed me once more before climbing onto the mattress and crawling down my body.

He slowly unzipped my boots and pulled each one off, removed my socks and kissed the entire surface of my feet. Bastian made the simplest act incredibly erotic by taking the time to admire and love on my body. His fingers deftly unsnapped my jeans and peeled them down my legs, taking my underwear along with them. He hungrily eyeballed my cock, tracking the bead of pre-cum that slid down my length. In one smooth movement, he bent forward and collected the drop on his tongue, humming at the flavor as his eyes slid closed. I made a mental note to ask Ben to help me get an appointment scheduled at the clinic downstairs to make sure I was free of anything I could pass on to my lover. I craved to let him drink my seed and swallow his down as well. I wanted to taste him. I wanted him to take me without protection and mark me inside as his. But until that appointment, I'd do nothing to put him in harm's way.

    Bastian lifted my sweater from my body, tickling the smooth skin of my chest as he went. "Your body gets more breathtaking every time I see it," he crooned. He kissed a line from my navel to my collarbone, stopping to swirl his tongue over my pointed nipples as I moaned and arched up into him. He took my lips again, kissing me deeply and slowly until I was breathless.

"I need to see you too, Bastian. Please," I begged, pulling at his suit jacket. He stood next to the bed and quickly removed his tie, jacket and shirt, tossing them onto the floor. He toed out of his shoes and socks before quickly dropping his pants and boxers, finally unveiling his gorgeous body.

My mouth watered at the sight of him, but my anxiety also rose; his cock was even bigger than I remembered. Bigger than I'd ever taken before. Though I'd had a couple of days to relax and heal, I was unsure if I could take him without pain. But I wanted this; wanted *him*.

Bastian sat on the edge of the bed and caressed up my chest and down my arms, soothing me as if he could feel my unease. "Milo, I would never do anything that you are unsure of or that may harm you."

"I know, Papi." It would go against everything he'd shown me and everything he was. I took a deep breath to calm my nerves while Bastian reached into his nightstand and pulled out a new box of condoms; a *huge* box of 144 love gloves. I pursed my lips to keep from laughing. "Do you think you have enough?" I teased.

Bastian gave me a worried look before turning his gaze on the box and then back to me. "I can get more."

I couldn't hold my chuckle back any longer. "God, I love you."

A goofy grin crossed his lips. "I love you too." He fished out a foil packet and ripped it open. He studied the latex for a minute and nodded like he'd solved some big mystery. Then he steadied the condom in his fingers before placing it over the tip of *my* dick and rolling it down. My face contorted into a look of utter bewilderment. "Is this okay? I thought perhaps you would prefer this for our first time. I don't want you to experience any discomfort; only pleasure."

My heart grew too large for my chest. "Bastian, have you ever done this before? Bottomed, I mean?" He shook his head no and my pulse raced. It was so special to be sharing one of his firsts; one of *our* firsts, seeing as I'd never topped before either. "And you're sure about this?"

"Absolutely. Cielito, I long to be with you in a way that leaves no room for fear or uncertainty. I only wish for your pleasure and to give you an experience that you shall remember for the rest of your life."

"Damn." I couldn't spin beautiful phrases like Bastian, but his answering smile told me he didn't mind. "Do you have lube? I don't want to hurt you."

Bastian nodded. "It's also in the nightstand. I apologize I didn't know your preferred brand. I asked Sam to purchase what he thought to be the best for us." I would have thought it was odd that he asked his friend to buy lube so we could have sex, but having met Sam, I was positive he didn't mind.

I opened the drawer and bit my cheek to keep from laughing. A gallon sized pump bottle of lube was stashed on its side. I had to wriggle and tug the container out of the nightstand because of how tightly it fit inside the drawer. When I finally got it free, I put it on top of the stand and *did* laugh at how huge and ridiculous and so totally Sam it was.

"Is something wrong?" Bastian asked seriously.

"Not at all; I'll have to remember to thank him for this."

Bastian nodded and reached out to take my hand. He stroked his thumb across my fingers and the look of love and need in his eyes erased any amusement from my mind. He positioned himself in the middle of the bed and laid back, bending his knees and pulling his heels back to his ass, offering himself to me. I nearly filled the condom at the sight.

Because Bastian's bed was so large, I couldn't climb on top of him at the center and reach the nightstand at the same time, so I hefted the huge bottle onto the mattress beside him before crawling over to him and settling on my knees between his.

The view was even better close up. Papi's long, curly black hair fanned out around his face and draped over his pillow, making him look like a dark angel. His thick, muscled chest heaved with excited breaths and his enormous cock dripped steadily, forming a puddle on his stomach. His balls hung heavy and low, and beneath them was Bastian's perfect, untouched pucker, which fluttered and flinched with anticipation.

I fought the urge to dive right in, determined to give my lover a more romantic experience than that. I lowered my much smaller body onto Bastian's, feeling like I was climbing a sexy mountain. I pressed our lips together, kissing and tasting him until my cock was throbbing with need. I licked down his neck and onto his chest. He'd always been so loving and tender with my body and I wanted to return the favor; to show him how I felt about him.

Bastian's breath caught when I flicked my tongue across his nipple. I pressed into the bead as I circled against it. His moans told me he enjoyed my touch, and I wanted to give him more. I pinched his other nipple between my fingers and rolled the flesh as I sucked against his sensitive skin.

Bastian fisted the blanket beneath him and moaned. "Mi sangre arde por ti!" *Damn, I really need to learn some Spanish.* I was positive the one year I took in school didn't cover the naughty words he was saying. I pinched his nipple harder between my fingers as my teeth bit gently into his other one. "Fuck!" *Okay, that I understood.* I nibbled his light brown disc as I plucked and squeezed the other. Bastian cursed and groaned and I could tell my big man liked a firm touch. I didn't think it was possible for me to hurt him, but I wouldn't take any chances.

"Tell me if it's too much," I whispered, and Bastian shivered when my breath hit his wet nipple.

"Not possible," he moaned, arching up further into my touch. "I want it all, Milo; give me everything."

Jesus. I reluctantly released his skin to kiss a line down his torso. I nipped at each mound of muscle and ran my tongue through every valley until I reached his cock; firm, tall and weeping. I kissed his tip, pulling back a long string of pre-cum attached to my lips when I raised my head. Bastian's gaze darkened as he watched me lick my lips to capture the fluid.

"Dios mio," he breathed as his eyes rolled back. I gripped his thick base in my fist, pressed my flattened tongue to his angry red crown, and painted my taste buds with his salty sweet flavor. Bastian trembled and cursed as I laved his cock. I licked down his length and over every inch of his sack, sucking each ball into my mouth and flicking against it with the tip of my tongue.

I stretched my jaw to take Bastian's fat tip between my lips and sucked it like a lollipop. I couldn't take his whole length into my throat without being uncomfortable, and

I knew he wouldn't want that, so I gave all of my attention to his sensitive head. I sucked hard around the mushroom tip until my cheeks hollowed and I pumped my fist over his shaft.

"Cielito, your mouth is heaven," he crooned, sinking his hands into my hair. Unlike the men I'd encountered before, Bastian didn't push down or force himself further inside; he just wanted to touch me. I quickly flicked my tongue across his slit as I pumped my wrist faster. When I pushed the tip of my tongue inside his slash, Bastian's back arched off of the bed. "Milo, I'm not going to last."

I wasn't ready for this to end before I made love to my gorgeous man, so I begrudgingly pulled my lips from his cock and released my hand. I pumped a puddle of lube into my palm and looked to Bastian for permission. He nodded eagerly and spread his legs wider.

Both of us moaned when I touched a slick finger to his pucker. I couldn't pull my gaze away as I circled his wrinkled flesh. His muscles were thick and tight beneath my fingers, so I massaged them thoroughly, giving him the love and attention I'd never had. I wanted him to only have positive memories of this moment.

Once his flesh thinned and loosened beneath my touch, I slid the tip of my finger into his hole. Before I could ask if he was okay, Bastian moaned and pushed down, sinking my entire digit into his warm channel. I slowly pulsed my finger back and forth. Each time I pulled back, his body gripped me and sucked me back inside.

I added a second finger, swirling and separating my digits, stretching out his tight entrance. When I circled across the top of his channel, Bastian's hips flew up off of the bed. "Santa mierda!" I blinked at him with huge eyes, unsure if that was good or bad. "More, Milo; *please*!"

Okay, it was good. I pressed the top of his passage again, this time feeling a soft, rubbery patch of skin. When I rubbed the patch, Bastian's legs quivered and he moaned a string of words I didn't understand but they still made me blush. I pressed both fingers against the spot and grinded them back and forth until his words became one continuous moan.

"Cielito, please; I need you inside me," he managed to say between ragged breaths. "I need you, my love." Anxious to give him anything and everything he needed, I withdrew my fingers and pumped my shaking hands full of lube. I hissed when I ran my slick hands over my latex-covered dick, and grimaced when I realized I'd gotten way too much liquid as it dripped all over the bed.

I decided too much was better than not enough, and didn't try to wipe any away. Besides that, if I touched my cock again, it might explode, and I wanted to do that inside Bastian. I lined my tip up with his stretched hole and pushed in gently. Once again, Bastian bared down and swallowed me up in one movement. My eyes went cross at the warm bliss when I was fully seated inside him.

"Is this okay?" I asked once I got myself under control.

"It is exquisite," he answered, his lust-blown eyes staring right through me.

I slowly pulled back until just my tip was inside him before pushing fully inside. After a few more thrusts and getting throaty moans from my lover, I picked up the pace. I backed my hips away and snapped them forward, burying myself to the hilt over and over again as Bastian's head whipped from side to side.

I gripped his hips and moved faster, harder until I was fucking him at a frantic speed. The smooth heat of his channel hugged against my dick perfectly, threatening to milk me dry. And god, how I wanted it.

Sweat beaded across my brow and my breaths were shallow and rapid. The underused muscles of my back and hips burned as I thrust into him, but I didn't dare stop. My hands tightened on Bastian's sides. He peeled them from his skin and held them firmly in his own, giving me new leverage to plow into my lover. Holding hands with Bastian as I ravaged his hole gave a tender touch to the experience and made my heart sing.

"Cielito, I'm going to come!" Bastian cried out, and I barreled through my sore muscles and aching body to grant him release. My hands squeezed his as I fucked him wildly. A roar ripped from his chest as his untouched dick engorged and erupted over his abdomen, painting thick white stripes over his golden skin.

His ass squeezed around me so firmly I could only pulse my hips back and forth a few inches. Pressure built inside my pelvis and my balls drew up. My cock swelled. "Papi!" I exploded, pumping the condom full of my seed as my body quaked.

My face tingled as I caught my breath and my pulse slowly came back down. I opened my eyes to find Bastian looking at me with such love and wonder, I had to blink hard to keep tears at bay.

"That was amazing," he whispered, reaching his hands up to comb my wild hair from my face. "I love you so much, Milo."

"I love you too, Bastian." I leaned forward to take his lips in a slow, tender kiss. When I released him, I smiled at the sight of his jizz splattered up his stomach. My sexy man had gotten so worked up and felt so good, I hadn't even had to touch him to get him off. Damn if that didn't make me feel proud. "Let me get something to clean you up." I held the base of the condom as I pulled out of Bastian's well-loved hole. I took a step toward the bathroom, but stopped. "Actually, would you want to take a shower with me?"

A huge grin spread across his face. "I like that idea much better."

For the next half hour, Bastian and I scrubbed each other, stole kisses and cuddled under the water. He changed the settings on the jets so the streams pounded and relaxed my sore muscles. He massaged shampoo into my hair before carefully rinsing it out, making sure none of it got in my eyes. I decided I never wanted to shower alone again.

"Are you getting hungry for dinner?" Bastian asked after we'd patted each other dry with fluffy towels and *somehow* ended up back in bed, snuggling under the covers. "I will cook anything you like or would be happy to take you out."

"How would you feel about just eating the leftovers from the pizza place here in bed while we watch TV? That way we can stay naked and...maybe do that again?" My cheeks flushed at admitting I was ready to make love to Bastian again so soon, but his huge grin told me he was okay with that.

"You are full of great ideas today, Cielito."

Chapter Seven

Bastian

I knew I was being extremely creepy as I lay staring at Milo, but I couldn't help it. He was just so beautiful. Plus, he was still sleeping, so it's not like he knew how creepy I was being. Or that I'd *been* creepy for the past four hours. I smiled as I looked over his gorgeous body and remembered how amazing it felt when he was inside me for the first *and* second time yesterday.

"I can feel you looking at me," Milo whispered, his mouth twitching up into a grin.

"I'd say I was sorry, but I cannot lie to you, my love." I brushed his bangs off of his forehead and smiled as his pretty blue-gray eyes opened and danced with humor.

"Do I want to know how long you've been watching me drool?"

"You don't drool," I insisted as I wiped a crusty patch of dried saliva from his chin, making him laugh.

Milo scooted closer to me to rest his head on my chest. I immediately wrapped him up in my arms. "How do you feel today?" he asked quietly. "Are you sore?"

"Deliciously so." Since our lovemaking was an act of pleasure and not punishment, my body didn't heal itself, and I was thankful I could still feel the pleasant stretch and burn Milo gave me.

He raised his head and looked at me with concern. "Oh god, did I hurt you? I guess we shouldn't have done it twice. I'm so sorry, Papi; I never meant to-"

I pecked his lips to quiet his worries. "Trust me, I'm not complaining. It's perfect."

He settled down again, nuzzling deeper into my hold. "*This* is perfect. I wish we could spend the whole day together being lazy."

"Your wish is my command."

"Don't you have to go in to work?"

"I took the day off." Actually, Dante insisted I take some time off to make sure my mate was settled in, and to hopefully complete our bonding soon. He was an impeccable boss, leader and friend.

"Really?" Milo asked excitedly. I nodded and he squeezed me tighter. "Thank you."

"You're most welcome, Cielito. Besides laziness, is there anything else you'd like to do today?"

He rolled to his side, propping his head on his hand as he looked at me. "Well, I had an idea, but I wanted to check with you first to make sure it was okay."

"What is it?"

"I'd like to get together with Sam and Ben again, and Dante as well, especially since I haven't got to spend much time with him. Do you think it'd be okay to ask them all over for a movie night or something?"

My heart swelled. It meant so much that Milo was growing close to my friends, and making them his friends as well. "I think it's a wonderful idea to get everyone together. But Cielito, you never have to check with me if you want to have people over. This is your home. If I have to work and you'd like to spend time with Ben and Sam or anyone else, please call them. I want you to have everything your heart desires."

Milo swallowed thickly. "You know, I never thought I'd be glad that I almost got stabbed in a filthy alleyway, but it turned out to be the best thing that ever happened to me because I met you."

His words filled me with love and happiness. I leaned in and gave him a gentle kiss; or what I meant to be a gentle kiss. Milo had other plans, deepening the kiss and wrapping his arms around my neck to pull me with him as he rolled onto his back. I kept only enough weight on him so he could feel pressure and warmth. I was sure he could also feel my cock as it filled and hardened against him, especially since we hadn't had clothes on since yesterday afternoon.

"This is the best way to wake up," Milo said breathlessly as I kissed down his neck. Once again, I found his pulse point easily. I licked against the flesh as it vibrated against my tongue, beckoning me to bite down. I didn't; I couldn't, but I *did* allow myself to suck his skin into my mouth and draw up a beautiful purple love bite. "That feels so good, Papi," Milo moaned. His dick was hard and throbbing now as well, and he humped against me, rubbing our heated erections together. I rolled my hips down to meet him and to provide him friction.

Pre-cum oozed from both of us and slicked our path. Milo's hips thrust even quicker as he whimpered and trembled against me. My fangs dropped and I grazed them along my mate's flesh, enjoying the tingle.

"God, when you suck on my neck it feels like you're sucking my dick," he panted. I allowed the tip of my fang to prick his skin and lapped up the single drop of blood that seeped out. It was sweet and warm and caused my mouth to water as if it were crying for more. "Yes, Papi!" he screamed, furiously humping into me. "Bite me! Please, it feels amazing!" My fangs ached with longing. "Please!"

I couldn't fight my desires any longer, especially knowing my beloved shared them. I pierced Milo's flesh with my sharp fangs and sucked in a mouthful of his warm, butterscotch blood. I moaned at the delicious flavor as my eyes rolled back in my head.

"Oh my god!" Milo screamed, grabbing the back of my head and shoving it harder against his throat. I crashed my pelvis to his, trapping our cocks together and feverishly rocking my hips. My lover's body shook as he cried aloud. "Yes, Bastian! Oh fuck, Papi! I'm gonna-" Before he could finish his sentence, Milo's dick erupted between us, covering both of our abdomens in hot, sticky liquid.

As I drank from my beloved, relishing the feel of his life force sliding down my throat, Milo continued to pump his seed between us, whining and whimpering in ecstasy. My balls drew tight to my body and I too exploded, painting my lover with my seed. The smell of our combined release in the air and the taste of him on my tongue made me dizzy with euphoria.

Full of my mate's blood, I felt stronger, keener and more vibrant than ever before. My senses were sharper and my body hummed with energy. I slowly retracted my fangs and licked over the small wounds in Milo's neck as he shivered and moaned again. His skin closed and formed a beautiful mating scar he would wear for all time. We were only half-bonded, but now every paranormal being on earth would know this perfect man belonged to me.

"Oh, Papi," Milo whispered. I drew my eyes from his throat to his blissed-out glassy expression. "The things you do to me." His mouth tipped into a lop-sided satisfied smile. "Amazing."

"You are the truly amazing one, Cielito." I brushed his hair away from his sweaty forehead before dropping a kiss onto his flushed skin. "I love you always."

"I love-" his words broke off as a yawn took over his lips. "I'm sorry; I'm just so sleepy all of the sudden." My feedings would take a toll on Milo until his body adjusted.

Soon, he would have a greater blood volume and higher stamina.

"You rest, my love, and I will be here when you wake." Milo slowly nodded as his eyes drifted shut. Within moments, his breathing evened out and he was fast asleep. I rose to retrieve a warm cloth from the bathroom. I cleaned my mate and then myself before climbing back into bed with Milo, snuggling him close and tucking the blankets around him to make sure he was warm. I was creepy once more as I stared at him, studying his beauty until my phone rang on the nightstand beside me. I picked it up and smiled at Ben's name on the screen.

"Good morning Ben."

"Good morning, Bastian!" he answered cheerfully. "I'm calling because Sam and I are getting ready to watch a movie while Dante is working and we were hoping Milo wanted to join us. I made a bunch of snacks for the day!"

"He's making me watch a nature documentary," Sam pouted over the line. "He lured me in with food and then sprung a fucking monkey movie on me. Send Milo up here; he knows what movies are good. Maybe if it's two against one, Ben will fold."

"No," the little sweetheart stated firmly. "I watched people getting hacked up with chainsaws yesterday, so today you guys can watch cute little monkeys with me."

I smiled at his words and his thoughtfulness. "Thank you so much for thinking of my mate, but he is resting now."

"Aw, is he a late sleeper?" Ben asked. "We can wait for him."

"What, and put off this *fabulous* monkey movie?" Sam teased. "How will I survive?" A slap sounded over the line and Sam snorted. I was sure Ben just smacked his friend, which Sam seemed to thoroughly enjoy. I wasn't sure I'd ever understand those two.

"Thank you, but go ahead and enjoy your film," I replied. "He will probably be asleep for a while. I...I just fed." There was no sense in hiding what just happened from my friends, considering they were well versed on the topic. Plus, I wanted to gloat a little.

"Holy shit!" Sam exclaimed. "That was quick. I can't wait to tell princey-poo you two bonded so quickly and make him feel like a wuss for putting things off with Ben."

"You'll do no such thing!" Ben interjected. "My Dante's timing was perfect and so was our bonding."

"Your bonding is old news. I want to hear about Bastian and Milo's bonding. Bastian, tell me all about it. I want all the sexy details; and talk slowly so I can really picture it."

Ben muttered 'gross' at the same time a growl sounded in my chest. "You shall not picture my mate in such a manner! And besides...we're only half bonded," I admitted. "I fed from my beloved in a moment of passion, but he does not yet know of my identity."

"For fuck's sake," Sam murmured as Ben gasped.

"Bastian, you have to tell him! You can't be feeding from him when he doesn't know what it means!"

Guilt burst in my chest at Ben's words. I'd been so focused on my happiness and pleasuring Milo that I wasn't looking at things clearly. I'd fed from him; taken sustenance and vitality from him without being honest about what it meant. "You're right," I answered sadly, placing my hand over Milo's head and pushing my apology and love into him as he slept. "I need to tell him, but I'm nervous about his reaction. I never want him to think I just want to use him like Jerome did. I need him to understand what all he is to me."

"I'm sure he knows," Ben replied quietly. "But I can also see why you're worried." He let out a long breath. "Maybe a little more time to ease him into things isn't such a bad idea, especially since you've already fed. But you can't do it again until you guys talk."

"You're right." Ben was wise beyond his years and loyal to the core. His level head and caring soul were a blessing to our coven and its rule.

"And we will do everything we can to make sure he knows he is wanted here," he added. "That way when you disclose to him, he will know he is important to and loved by all of us; that even though you *need* him, we also *want* him."

"Babe, you're the best," Sam told him seriously, and I had to agree. "So Bastian, if you're not ready to nut up and tell him yet, why don't we all do something together tonight to make him feel included? Milo said he wanted to hang out with everyone."

"That's a great idea, Sam!" Ben squealed.

"I've been known to have them every now and then."

"Yes Sam, that's a lovely idea. But we will need to go somewhere that my beloved feels secure."

"He'll be secure anywhere; he'll have three badass vampires with him! And..you know...Ben."

"Hey!" Ben exclaimed, sounding offended.

"Babe, you know I love you, but you're just not scary. You're cute, funny, and have a sexy ass, but you're not scary."

"Aw, Sam, thank you!" I rolled my eyes at the young pair even though they couldn't see it. "Ooh, I know! The coven owns a bowling alley downtown. I'll ask Dante to close it to anyone who aren't members, and have him post security at the entrance. How does that sound?"

"Bowling?" Sam asked, sounding unimpressed. "I was thinking like a strip club or gay bar or something." Ben and I both growled at him, making him laugh. "God, you two are whipped."

"You wish you were *being* whipped," Ben teased.

"Fuck yeah I do."

"Okay, well, if this conversation is over, I'll be going now," I interrupted, uncomfortable with the turn things had taken. "Ben, bowling sounds delightful. Let Milo and I know the details later and we shall all ride together. Goodbye." I didn't give him time to respond before closing the call.

I went back to studying my lover while thoughts of how much I loved him and how I should go about telling him my secret swirled in my head.

Chapter Eight

Bastian

"You look gorgeous, Cielito," I breathed as Milo stepped out of our bedroom wearing ripped black jeans, his boots, and a long sleeved olive green top that laced up the front. His sleeves were pushed up to show the bracelet I gave him. I loved the way his new clothes reflected his inner strength and gave him newfound confidence.

"Thank you," he answered with a smile. "You look sexy too, Papi." Since we were going out for a casual night on the town, I dressed down in dark jeans and a black t-shirt. I was also wearing black boots I'd found in my closet. They weren't as trendy as Milo's, but he still loved them on me. I gave my beloved a quick, fierce kiss, but was interrupted when a knock sounded on the door.

"Why the fuck are you wearing a tie?" I heard Sam's voice ask from the other side of the wood when we approached.

"Because I wanted to look presentable," Dante answered in an irritated tone. "I want Bastian's beloved to know we are happy to have him with us."

"By looking like a douche? Nobody wears a tie to go bowling!"

"*I* think you look very handsome," Ben countered.

"Thank you, Amorcito; as do you."

"Now see *that* I agree with," Sam interrupted. "Nice job on the short sweater, babe. God, I can't wait to see those fat cheeks in action when you're tossing balls. I'm getting chubby just thinking about-" his words were cut off as a growl and a choking sound pierced the air. When Sam croaked out "Harder!", a second, smaller growl entered the mix and the choking sounds intensified. I could only imagine the fuckery going on beyond my front door. I looked to Milo to see his eyes were wide with concern.

"*Stop it!*" I vampire whispered to Dante and Sam. "*Please! You're scaring my mate.*"

"*I apologize, amigo,*" Dante offered as the hall went quiet. "*Forgive me; I will refrain from such actions and I'm sure Sam will be on his best behavior for the rest of the night.*"

"Yes, Mom."

Before they could get riled up again, I threw open the front door and was greeted by three widely grinning faces. I rolled my eyes and motioned for the three stooges to enter.

"Good evening," Dante told Milo with a bow. "It's an honor to see you again."

"Thank you, Dante. I'm glad we're getting to spend some time together."

"Hey, Milo!" Ben greeted, wrapping my mate in a hug.

"Hey, Ben." He patted his friend's back before Ben returned to Dante's side, and Sam took his place.

"You look hot," Sam said as he too hugged my mate. He only rolled his eyes when I growled. "Don't you think he looks hot?"

"Well of course I do," I huffed. "But you can keep such opinions to yourself."

Milo stood on his tiptoes and kissed my cheek to calm me. "Thanks, Sam. You look nice too," my mate offered sweetly. Sam *actually* looked ridiculous in tight pants and a see-through shirt, but I kept that thought to myself.

"Shall we go?" Dante asked, looking around the group. We all nodded and rode the elevator down to the lobby. When we stepped out, we nearly bumped into Dmitri, who was carrying a bouquet of roses and a large gift bag.

"Good evening, Dmitri," Dante offered with a smile. "Heading home to Sondra?"

"Yes, sir. We're having a bit of a celebration; today marks two weeks since our bond...um, wedding," he caught himself as he looked to Milo.

"Aw, that's so sweet!" Ben crooned. "Congrats!"

"Thank you, Master Ben," he replied with a bow. "It was lovely to see you all, but if you will excuse me, I must be off." He bowed once more before taking our place in the elevator.

"I like Dmitri," my mate smiled once the doors closed. "He seems really nice."

"Yeah, and his rim jobs could make a Cadillac jealous," Sam replied dreamily. "Sondra's a lucky bitch."

I had no idea what he was talking about, but the way Milo's eyes widened and his cheeks flushed, I figured it was naughty. Seeing as it was Sam talking, I was sure of it. I wrapped my arm around Milo's shoulders and escorted him toward the front door as I shot a glare at Sam, who just winked at me.

The ride downtown was quite enjoyable. Sam *was* on his best behavior, as he and Ben talked to Milo and asked him a hundred questions about himself, his likes and dislikes. Sam was excited to hear that my mate liked heavy metal music, which I knew already because of the store he'd enjoyed at the shopping mall. Ben turned on the radio and found a station that played the genre so that he, Sam and Milo could "rock out" together; meaning they violently bounced their heads around to the pounding beat. It didn't look like it felt pleasant, but the smiles on all three faces said they were enjoying themselves. The look on Dante's face said he hated the music; it was much different than the classical style he preferred, but he kept his thoughts to himself.

When we reached the bowling alley, my Milo was keyed up, grinning brightly, and looking to be having the time of his life before we even entered the building. "It fills me with joy to see you so happy, Cielito," I whispered into his ear as we walked down the sidewalk.

He stopped to face me and wrap his arms around my waist. "I *am* happy. God, Bastian, I never thought I could be this happy. Thank you." He lurched up on his tiptoes as I bent down, and we fell into a heated kiss. Our tongues were quick to battle and taste, and his hands slipped from my hips onto my buttocks.

"Ow, *ow*!" Sam yelled, reminding us we weren't alone. Milo and I separated and looked to Sam, who was rudely thrusting his hips. "Right here on the fucking sidewalk? I like your style, Milo." Before I could respond with what was sure to be a threat, my mate laughed and grabbed my hand, pulling me inside the building.

The area was full but not packed with many of our coven members. Those whom hadn't seen Milo and I together stared, smiled or offered quiet well wishes. I puffed up with pride and pulled my beloved closer to my side.

Since Dante owned the place, we didn't have to pay, and he didn't mention the questionable, smelly-looking shoes that were lined up behind the counter. We simply made our way to the lane he'd reserved for us. We picked our balls (which Sam turned into an endless string of off-color jokes) and entered our names on the monitor above us.

"*So,*" Sam whispered in a volume Milo couldn't hear as he sat beside me, "*I take it from the little display on the sidewalk you* two have dipped into the condoms I brought you?"

"I don't believe that's any of your business. And yes, we've used a few." I couldn't pass up an opportunity to brag that I'd been with such a gorgeous creature.

"*Really?*" Sam looked over at Milo, who was placing his ball in the return, and back at me. "*Why isn't he walking like a damn cowboy then? I know what kind of heat you're packing in those pants.*" I narrowed my eyes at him, but before I could say anything, his face broke out in a wicked grin. "Holy shit!"

The rest of our group hurried over to us. "What's wrong?" Milo asked, looking concerned.

"You tapped that?" Sam asked, excitedly pointing at me. Half of the damn crowd in the building turned to look at us. Milo's cheeks burned red as he gave a slight nod. "Holy shit!" Sam repeated.

"Wait, you were on top?" Ben asked curiously. Feeling my mate's embarrassment, I stood and pulled him close to me. He gave another small incline of his head to Ben. "How was it?"

"You don't have to answer that, Cielito," I whispered to him. "I'm sorry; my friends - *our* friends - can be quite intrusive."

"It's okay," he whispered back before raising his head to look at Ben and Sam, who both looked hungry for details. "It was amazing. Bastian was wonderful and took such good care of me, and it was the best experience of my entire life."

"Aww," Ben gushed, folding his hands over his heart. "That's beautiful. Osito, would you ever want *me* to be on top?" Dante's eyes darkened as he stared at his husband. I knew they were having a silent mental conversation by the way Ben giggled and nodded his head quickly.

"Shall we bowl?" I asked, looking for a change of subject to break the tension.

Dante, Sam and I proved to be great at the sport, given our keen eyesight, speed and strength. We each rolled strikes during the first four frames. Milo was quite gifted as well, though he'd never bowled before. Poor Ben was having quite a bit of trouble. After his first three frames of gutterballs, Dante placed bumpers in the gutters for his husband on his turn. Even with them, Ben only knocked over four pins. His shoulders slumped in defeat, but after Dante showered his face with kisses and whispered naughty promises of consolation in his ear, Ben perked back up.

"Sam, you're up," Ben called once he was feeling better. "Sam? Where's Sam?"

We all looked around, and it didn't take us long to find him across the room flirting with two other vampires. He was laughing at something they said while caressing their chests. He caught us looking at him and jogged over.

"It's your turn," Ben pointed out.

"Can you roll for me, babe? Actually, sorry, but you're kind of terrible. Bastian, will you roll for me? I need to take a quick trip to the Eiffel Tower." He flicked his eyebrows and jogged off again, collecting the two men and leading them toward the restroom.

"He said I was terrible," Ben pouted.

"*He's* terrible," Dante countered, making Ben giggle and Milo smile. "And what does he mean he's going to the Eiffel Tower?" Ben shrugged at the question and they both looked to me. I was clueless as well.

"Um..." Milo started and cleared his throat before continuing, "It's a...position." Ben's eyebrows raised in interest. "So, assume Sam is in the middle like this," He held his hand horizontally flat, "With one guy behind him and one guy in front of...his face..." His cheeks flushed but he pressed on, "The two guys hold hands above him and they kind of make an 'A' shape or triangle...or-"

"The Eiffel Tower," the three of us finished for him and he nodded.

"Oh my," Ben whispered. Considering a third person was involved in the position, he didn't ask Dante about his interest. "Um, Bastian, do you want to roll his turn?" he asked, changing the subject again.

I picked up a ball and winked at Ben before placing it in the gutter and rolling it down. "Oops." When I repeated the action for the second shot, Ben giggled and gave me a high five on my way back to my seat.

"You're a good friend," Milo asserted before kissing my cheek. I sat up straighter and pulled him close to my side.

For the next five frames, I rolled gutterballs for Sam, and Dante and I cuddled our mates between turns. Sam finally returned, looking debauched and reeking of sex and sweat. He scoffed as he caught sight of his score on the monitor.

"What the hell, Bastian?"

"Maybe you should have kept your hands on your *own* balls," Milo quipped, making Ben, Dante and me laugh. Sam's face exploded into a grin.

"That was a good one." He held his hand up and my mate slapped his against it.

After we bowled our last frame, Ben did a happy dance at squeaking out a fourth place victory over Sam since I'd purposefully tanked his score. Sam pulled out his wallet and waved some money at Ben as he danced, and Dante barely stopped himself from choking the insufferable vampire in front of my mate, though he couldn't keep his eye from twitching violently.

Milo laughed at the scene playing out in front of him, and my pulse raced at the lovely sound. My beloved was enjoying himself, his life, and his friends, and that was more than I could ever ask for. He turned his beautiful smile on me before pulling me into a long, slow kiss. He leaned close and whispered in my ear, "My heart is full." I nearly swooned at the perfection of the moment and hearing my own words and thoughts repeated; Milo knew how much it meant to me.

"Let's play another round!" Ben requested.

"Yeah, I need to dish out some payback for that shit show," Sam agreed. "What do you say, Milo?" He, Dante and Ben all turned hopeful eyes on my mate, who nodded vigorously.

"Game on."

Chapter Nine

Milo

"Please don't do this!" I begged Jerome as he cocked the gun he had pointed at Bastian's head. My boyfriend was strapped to a chair in Jerome's kitchen. Andre and Marcus grinned wickedly as they looked on.

"You did this," Jerome snarled. "You've been parading around town like you're something better than the shit on my shoe. You ran off, spitting in my face after I gave you everything, you ungrateful little faggot. You thought you wouldn't have to answer for it?"

"You gave him nothing," Bastian spat. "How could you harm such a precious creature? You are foul and wicked and deserve to burn in hell!"

Jerome slammed the butt of his gun against Bastian's face. My lover shook his head as his eyes tried to refocus. "Shut your fucking mouth!" He pressed the barrel to Bastian's temple. "Say goodbye to lover boy."

The door burst open from behind me and Sam, Ben and Dante barreled into the room. My heart filled with hope that Bastian and I might escape this. Jerome pointed his gun at my friends and shot three rounds, dropping them all to the ground. I screamed and clutched at their lifeless bodies as blood painted the kitchen floor.

"And now for you," Jerome growled, turning the pistol back on Bastian. "Tell me; was it worth it? Was fucking this little whore worth losing all of your friends? Your life?"

"Yes," Bastian answered easily as a tear streamed down his cheek. "You are worth everything, Cieli-" his words were cut off when Jerome pulled the trigger.

"No!" I screamed as tears flooded my face. "Please, god, no!" Two arms reached for me in the dark. I knew the end was here, but I didn't even fight it. I didn't want to live without Bastian and my friends. "Do it! Just fucking do it! Pull the trigger!" I begged.

"Milo! Milo, my love, *please* wake up!" I opened my eyes to find a terrified Bastian reaching out to me in the bed we shared. I threw my body against his and sobbed into his chest as he held me tighter than ever before. I ran my hands over every inch of his body I could reach, needing to know this was real. "I'm here, Cielito. I'm right here."

Panic washed over me again, and I wriggled my body free from his hold. He looked on in confusion as I leapt from the bed and stepped into the pants I'd tossed to the floor last night when we returned from our evening out with our friends. Bastian and I had pounced on each other as we entered the apartment, and scattered our clothes across the room as we clawed them off of one another before making passionate love.

"I have to go," I explained as I pulled on a shirt. I forcefully wiped my eyes dry; I didn't want him to see me upset. "I have to leave. I'm going to get you all killed."

"Milo, listen to me, you had a nightmare," Bastian said in a gentle tone, rising from the bed and holding his hands up in a placating gesture. "Everything is okay, my love. Everyone is okay."

"You won't be. I was so stupid to think I could get away from Jerome. I can't be here with you anymore, Bastian. He'll find us; he'll find *you*, and I can't let that happen. I won't be the reason you get killed. I'm not worth it." I stepped toward the door, but Bastian blocked my path.

"You are worth everything, Ciel-"

"No! Please don't say it," I begged. I clutched my chest at the memory of

Bastian's last words in my dream. Bastian looked so hurt and confused and it was ripping my heart out. "I love you so much, Bastian. Too much to let anything happen to you. I know it's hard, but you've got to let me go. It's the only way."

"Milo, I need to tell you something." I shook my head no, but didn't stop him from leading me back to the bed. I sat on the edge and Bastian kneeled in front of me, taking both of my hands in his. He took a deep breath and began, "I am not afraid of Jerome or anyone he is in contact with. I am stronger and faster than they could ever dream to be."

"I know you're strong, but I've told you they have lots of weapons at their fingertips and-"

"I am not afraid of their weapons either. It is very difficult for human weapons to harm me."

"You don't understand! They have...wait, what do you mean 'human weapons'?"

Bastian gave me an unsure smile. "The reason I am stronger and faster than humans is because I am *not* human...I'm a vampire."

"That's the most metal thing I've ever heard," I nodded. "Side note; you're delusional." I cocked my head at him. "Have you been talking to Ben?" Maybe the sweet man had shared his crazy thoughts on the paranormal with Bastian and convinced him of something equally as crazy.

"I know it sounds unbelievable, but it's true. I am three hundred and twenty eight years old, and I am destined to live forever. I came to America with Dante over one hundred years ago, and have served beside him as second in command to the vampire prince."

"You're saying Dante is a prince?" *My god, he's lost his damn mind. Am I still dreaming?* I reached down and pinched the shit out of my leg. *Ouch! No, I'm awake.*

"Yes, Cielito. He is prince of our people and the leader of our coven, and I am his Second. Everyone who resides here is part of our coven; everyone here is a vampire. Well, except for Ben. He is mated to Dante, and the consort to our prince. He has a hand in the running and ruling of our coven."

I closed my eyes and pinched the bridge of my nose. "I…" I didn't even know where to begin. I took a deep breath and looked at him once more. "Okay, so you're saying this whole building is full of vampires, including you, Dmitri, Sam and Dante?" Bastian nodded. "And sweet little Ben is mated to the master vampire prince?" He nodded once more. "And how much crack have you smoked this evening?"

"Please believe that what I'm telling you is true, Milo. I would never lie to you."

"So riddle me this; if I'm surrounded by vampires, why hasn't anyone tried to bite…" my face instantly paled and I reached up to touch the side of my neck. All I could see in the mirror when I admired the spot earlier was what I thought was an awesome hickey, but as my fingers trailed over the bruise, I felt two divots in my skin. "You bit me."

"I did. I bit you and drank your blood. I should have been forthcoming with you about my identity before I did so, and I apologize."

"You…drank my blood?" My stomach churned at the thought.

"Yes. I eat food like a human, but also need to drink blood to survive."

He fucking drank my blood. "So…you just run around biting people?" For some reason, the thought of Bastian drinking other people's blood was like a punch to the gut.

"No, Cielito. I drink bagged blood from the medical wing downstairs. Or, I used to. Now that I have you, I will only drink your blood. You are my mate. If I drink blood from anyone else, it will make me deathly ill."

"What do you mean by mate? You said Ben was Dante's mate. What does that mean?" It was the first of about a million questions I had.

"A mate is the most precious and treasured person in the vampire world. It is like a spouse in the human world, but the bond is deeper and unbreakable. Each vampire has one mate whom they will love and cherish for the rest of their life, which, as I told you, is eternal."

"Ben is human, though. And so am I." *Oh my god, I actually just said that. What the hell is happening right now?*

"Yes, but when a vampire mates with a human, that human takes on attributes of a vampire, including immortality."

"But we've mated like four times and I don't feel any different."

Bastian gave a soft chuckle. "Sweet Milo, to mate with a vampire, you must drink from each other."

"I have to drink your blood?" Bastian nodded and my stomach rolled again.

"Yes. And as your mate, I am unable to find any other person attractive or desire them in any way. I will crave only your body, touch, and blood for all of my days. I will do everything in my power to keep you safe and taken care of and I will fall even deeper in love with you every second of every day."

I'll admit that part of things sounded amazing, even if this night had taken a seriously fucked up turn. "So, I'm assuming you can prove this?" Part of me hoped he actually could.

"Yes." My heart sped up as he reached under the bed and pulled out a photo album. "These are photographs of myself throughout the years. The oldest ones date back to the very invention of photography, over one hundred fifty years ago."

I took the book with shaking hands and flipped through page after page of pictures. There were many of Bastian and Dante, who both looked exactly the same throughout time. They were convincing, but photos could be altered. I closed the cover and Bastian slid the book under the bed once more.

"And then of course, there are these." Bastian opened his mouth and my eyes widened as I watched his canine teeth grow to sharp fangs. They stayed long for a few seconds, and then he rectracted them until they were normal sized teeth again.

"Holy shit!" Even if Bastian had gotten prosthetic implants or something, I didn't see a way that he could make them do *that*. "Can...can you do that again?" His fangs lengthened again and I reached a finger toward them. Before I touched, I looked to Bastian's eyes for permission. He nodded and I gently pressed one of the elongated teeth as Bastian moaned. *He likes that?* I stroked the pad of my finger up and down the fang as my lover gripped the sheets of the bed on either side of me. "Holy shit," I repeated.

Bastian blinked his darkened eyes until they cleared once I'd removed my finger. He retracted his fangs and took my hands. "Do you believe me, Milo?"

"I think I have to." It was crazy and impossible, but I couldn't deny the evidence he'd shown me. It also explained all of the growling I always heard coming from Bastian and Dante. *Maybe that should have been a clue.*

"And do you think you can accept this of me?" Bastian asked, his eyes full of worry.

I searched my heart and mind, and only found one resounding answer. "Yes. I love you, Bastian. I don't care what you are; vampire, werewolf, fucking gremlin...I love *you*."

"I love you too." He wrapped me in a tight embrace. "I'm sorry I kept the truth from you, Milo."

"It's okay. I'm not sure I would have been ready to hear it before now."

He released me and pulled back to look into my eyes. "And now do you understand why I am not afraid of Jerome or his men?"

Shit. I forgot about them even though they were what started this whole conversation. "So you said you live forever...does that mean nothing can kill you?" I asked hopefully.

"No," he answered and my heart dropped. "I will perish if I do not drink blood. I can also be killed by being decapitated or having my heart pierced or removed."

Damn. None of those things were above what Jerome would do; he was heartless enough to kill anyone in any manner, and I knew for a fact he had good aim.

"Are you okay, Cielito?" Bastian asked, rubbing his hands up and down my arms.

"Yeah, I'm just a little overwhelmed, you know?"

"I'm so sorry, Milo. Is there anything I can do to help?"

"Actually...do you think Ben would mind talking with me? Since he's...you know...human..." *Shit, that sounds so weird.* "And has experience with all of this?"

"I think that's a wonderful idea."

"Okay, great. It's late, but I don't want to wait until morning. Do you think he'll be upset?"

"Not at all, Cielito."

"Okay, well...I'll head on up there."

"I will call Dante and let him know you are on your way. Would you like me to accompany you?"

"No, that's okay. I think I better go alone."

"Whatever you wish, my love. Thank you for understanding and accepting me for what I am." Bastian gave me a long, slow kiss, and I savored every moment, trying to memorize the feeling and taste, as it would be the last one we shared. I blinked hard to keep my tears away. "And you're sure you're okay?" he asked with narrowed eyes when we parted.

"Yep," I answered in a squeaky voice. "I'll go talk to Ben." I took a deep breath and looked deep into his eyes. "I love you, Bastian." Above all else, I needed him to know that.

"I love you too, Cielito. Always."

I gave him the best smile I could muster before leaving the bedroom, and then the apartment. Once I was in the elevator, I couldn't stop the tears from cascading down my face and neck as I hit the button for the ground floor. I meant what I told Bastian; I didn't care what he was. He was kinder than any human alive, and I loved him with everything inside me, which is why I had to leave. *He* may not be afraid of Jerome, but I sure as hell was. I knew what he could do if he ever found me, and seeing it in my dream made everything all too real. I wasn't so worried for myself, but I couldn't be the cause of anything happening to Bastian. Or my friends; when Ben was kidnapped, Dante, Sam and Bastian all went to his rescue. I knew they'd all fight to protect me, and I couldn't handle being the cause of their lives being cut short, especially when they were meant to last forever.

Since Bastian and I hadn't mated yet, surely he would be free to find another man. The thought gutted me, but he deserved it. He was the most perfect man alive and deserved a mate to share the rest of forever with. Someone who wouldn't put his life in danger simply by existing. I could only hope Bastian would forgive me for leaving and remember me fondly. I clutched my bare wrist, wishing I'd grabbed the bracelet Bastian gave me to have something to remember him by, though I knew I'd never forget him as long as I lived.

When I stepped out of the elevator, I saw Dmitri standing guard and surveying the empty lobby. I tried to sneak behind him, but of course he caught me.

"Good evening, sir," he greeted. His eyes filled with concern when they landed on my wet face. "Is everything okay?"

"Oh yeah," I lied, wiping my cheeks. "I just...had a bad dream." *Lame.* "I'm stepping out for a little fresh air."

"May I accompany you? It's quite late."

"No, no," I waved him off. "I'll just be right outside. But thank you."

"Of course, sir. If you change your mind, I'm here."

"Thanks, Dmitri." He smiled and bowed his head as I stepped into the cold night air. *I'll miss that guy.* I'd miss everyone. I wished I could have told my friends goodbye, but I knew they wouldn't understand or let me leave. My heart ached at the thought of what Bastian's reaction would be once he realized I was gone. The big man would lose his shit. But it was better than the alternative.

I stuck to the shadows even though this wasn't Jerome's usual beat. He and his men would surely be out looking for me by now, though. I rounded the corner of the building to walk down a dark alleyway. I had no plan besides hitchhiking as far away as I could get once I saw a trustworthy-looking motorist. For a moment, I thought about going back inside and just asking Bastian to take me away; to move to a new city or state where we may be safe, but that wasn't fair to him either. Especially since I knew he'd do it in a heartbeat. But his life was here. All of his friends and his *coven* was here. That had to be important. No, the best thing to do was to leave him alone completely so he could be free to get on with his life.

I froze in my tracks when I heard what sounded like a footstep in a puddle behind me. I threw myself against the wall into the shadows, but an echoing laugh told me it was too late.

"Where do you think you're going, faggot?"

I immediately recognized the voice; Andre. I peeled my trembling feet from the asphalt and ran as fast as I could toward the end of the alleyway. Though it was late, I hoped if I could make it to the road, a driver would be on the street and maybe scare off Andre.

A figure stepped in front of me at the end of the corridor. My heart leapt with hope until I got closer and made out Marcus's features. I skidded to a stop and looked behind me, only to see Andre closing in. I had nowhere to run.

Though I knew something horrific was about to happen to me, I couldn't help but be a little relieved. I'd made the right choice to leave. These men were right outside; so close to Bastian and my friends. It was only a matter of time before they would have gotten to them. At least this way, it would only be me. Unsure of what else to do, I dropped to my knees, balled up my body and covered my head, hoping to shield my most important organs.

"Get up!" Marcus barked as he lifted me to my feet by the collar of my shirt. "Jerome is looking for you."

"You don't have to do this," I murmured. "You can pretend you didn't find me. Hell, you can run away too." I was desperate for a solution that didn't result in my life ending tonight.

Andre laughed in my face when he caught up to us. "Run away? Why the fuck would we do that? We have everything we want with Jerome; food, drugs, women..."

"That's what happens when you do your job and make the boss money," Marcus added. "And when you don't, you become a cocksucking bitch."

Andre laughed at the other man's words before punching me hard in the stomach. I grunted and bent forward, clutching my abdomen. Marcus was quick to ram his fist across my jaw, sending me to the asphalt. My skull bounced off of the solid ground, and I saw stars dancing in my vision.

"God dammit, we were supposed to keep him conscious for Jerome!" Andre barked.

"Whatever, he'll come around before we get him back to the house."

I felt my body being lifted from the ground by rough hands before everything went black.

Chapter Ten

Bastian

I paced back and forth in the living room, anxiously waiting for Milo to come back home. I was pleased he went to talk to Ben; the man would be able to give valuable insight to my mate's situation. When I called Dante about ten minutes ago to let him know Milo was coming, he was congratulatory and ecstatic that my beloved was accepting of me, and gave his wishes for a quick bonding. When he woke Ben up to tell him, the little sweetheart squealed with delight and said he was looking forward to speaking with my beloved. He didn't care it was the middle of the night. My friends were incredible.

After the phone call, I dressed in my clothes from earlier in the night and came to my current position of wearing down the carpet in a path before the door. I wished Milo had let me go with him, but I understood his need for space. I dumped a lot of unbelievable information on him, and it would take his mind time to process everything.

My phone rang in my hand (I was clutching it tightly in case Milo needed me) and I looked at the screen. My brows furrowed when I saw the caller was Dmitri. I answered quickly, in case there was a situation downstairs that required my attention. He spoke before I even had the chance to say hello.

"Bastian, has Milo made it back to your apartment?"

I was confused; how did he know Milo wasn't here with me? "No, he's still with Ben and Dante."

"Did he just arrive with them?"

"No, he's been up there for about ten minutes."

"Sir, I spoke with Milo about ten minutes ago when he was stepping outside, and-"

"*What*? He went outside? Was he alone?" *What the hell is going on?*

"He looked quite upset, and when I questioned him, he said he had a bad dream and needed to clear his head outside. I tried to go with him, but he wanted to be alone. After several minutes, I grew concerned and looked outside but didn't see him. I made a lap of the premises but found no sign of him. I was hoping he slipped back inside while I was investigating. Something doesn't feel right, Bastian. I'm concerned for your mate's safety."

"Fuck!" I ended the call and dialed Dante, interrupting him as he answered. "Please tell me Milo is with you."

"He's not arrived yet," he replied. "We thought perhaps he was getting dressed. Is something wrong?"

"He's gone. He said he was going to talk to Ben, but Dmitri just called to say he left out the front door and that he's worried something happened to him."

"Dios mio. Meet me in the security room." I was out my door before he even finished the sentence. I rushed to the room of surveillance monitors which overlooked the entire outside of the property that Dante had installed after Hugo's followers crashed his and Ben's wedding. A breeze blew by me and suddenly Dante was at my side, carrying a terrified-looking Ben. Another gust of air delivered Sam to my opposite side. Peter, the young vampire whose job was to watch the monitors and contact security if anything looked suspicious, flinched and appeared taken aback by our abrupt entrance.

"Show us the tapes for the past ten minutes," I demanded. Peter nodded and rewound the security footage. He played it back slowly, and it didn't take long to see two men carrying Milo across the street and shoving him in the backseat of a silver SUV. "Why the fuck didn't you contact us?" I growled.

"I'm sorry; it looked like the guy just had too much to drink at the club and his friends were helping him out or something."

"That *guy* is my mate and those men want him dead, you useless fuck!"

Dante stepped between me and Peter before I could rip his head from his body. "You're off surveillance," he commanded. "Get Micah in here." Peter nodded again and rushed from the room.

"What the hell are we waiting for?" Sam asked.

"These," Ben answered. He'd climbed down from Dante's hold during the showdown with Peter to grab several bulletproof vests from the closet in the back of the room. He'd insisted Dante purchase them for his security team after the attack last month, claiming they could save lives because our hearts would be protected.

I gave a grateful nod to the man and Sam, Dante and I shrugged on our vests. To my surprise, Ben fastened into one as well. Dante gave a stern shake of his head, but Ben stood taller.

"He's my friend, Tay. I'm coming with you. I won't fight because I'll be a liability, but I'm coming, even if I have to stay in the car. I'm going to be there for him when he comes out of that terrible house." He gave me a sad smile, which I read like a book; he also wanted to be there for *me* if we were too late.

"My brave little love." Dante gave his husband a fierce, quick kiss.

"Let's go teach those stupid fuckers they don't mess with our friends," Sam added, cracking his knuckles.

We piled into the SUV with me behind the wheel. I had the most experience in driving like a bat out of hell without tipping the vehicle. I wasn't sure *exactly* where we were going, but had a general idea. Milo mentioned that the bookstore was near Jerome's house. I figured we could drive around the area until we saw the SUV from the video. It was all we had to go on.

I made it to the bookstore in record time, and everyone was on high alert. Our tires squealed as I wildly hooked around corners and blew through red lights. I clipped a road sign and lost a side mirror, but gave zero fucks.

"There it is!" Ben cried, pointing out the window to the silver SUV from the recording. It was parked in front of an unremarkable two story house that was set apart from any neighboring homes.

"Good work, babe," Sam replied, patting him on the back. Dante gave his mate another kiss as I whipped the vehicle onto the sidewalk and slammed it into park.

Sam, Dante and I exited the car, while Ben gave us all a tight smile from the backseat. "Be careful in there."

"Always," Dante replied. "Stay hidden, Benny. Don't open this door until you see us come out." Ben nodded as Sam shut the door. The click of the locks sounded and Dante breathed a sigh of relief knowing his mate was safe. I'd fight to my dying breath to be able to say the same.

The three of us sped across the street in a blur to the house, where Sam kicked in the front door. A dozen men jumped up from their seats at the sight of us. I scanned the room quickly and saw no sign of Milo.

Several of the men drew their weapons and shot an endless string of bullets at us. Most of them impacted against our vests, but the ones that pierced the flesh of our arms and legs slowly retreated from our bodies and clattered to the floor.

"What the fuck are you?" a wide-eyed man screamed as he continued to shoot, though his weapon caused us no harm besides a fleeting stinging sensation.

"Your worst nightmare, asshole," Sam replied before zipping over to the man at top speed and lifting him above his head. He let out a violent war cry as he pulled, separating the screaming man into two nearly perfect halves as blood rained over his head and shoulders. He flung the lifeless body to the floor and gave a wicked red-stained smile. "Who's next?"

The room erupted into chaos as the remaining men tried to flee. Dante and Sam dashed around the room, quickly taking out one by one in a limb ripping, blood splattering, screaming torrent of mayhem. Knowing the situation was under control, I bolted to the stairs and up, desperately searching for my mate.

*****

Milo

I woke up with a splitting headache. I tried to rub the tension from my forehead, but couldn't move my hand. I blinked until my fuzzy vision focused to look at my wrists, which were bound by a rope tied to a bedpost. A fruitless kick and a peek down my body confirmed my ankles were bound as well.

"Well, well, look who's up," Jerome's voice sounded from beside me. I turned my head to see him approaching the bed, a knife in the hand at his side. His cold black eyes stared through me, and his twisted smile showed the evilness within. I looked around to see if there was anyone else in the room with us. "It's just you and me," Jerome snarled, as if reading my thoughts. "Andre and Marcus wanted to watch me kill you, but since they couldn't follow the rules, now they just get to clean up afterwards." *Oh god.*

"We had an agreement," he continued, testing the sharpness of his blade with his fingertip. "You work for me, and I let you live. It was simple enough to understand. But what did you do? You ran off with some muscle for hire. Looks like your bodyguard didn't keep you safe though, huh?" He poked his bottom lip out in a mockingly sad expression.

"He's not my bodyguard; he's my boyfriend, and he'll come for me. He'll kill you and all of your men." God, I hoped that wasn't true. I hoped Bastian hadn't even noticed I was missing yet. I was only hoping to scare Jerome. He'd obviously seen Bastian, and knew he was a large, strong man who worked in security for the largest corporation around. Maybe if he was worried about Bastian coming for him, he'd let me go to save his own ass.

Or not. Jerome snarled and slashed his knife across my stomach, carving a deep gash into my flesh. Blood instantly soaked my shirt and I hissed at the stinging pain that bloomed over my skin and beneath. I was sure his blade had done more damage than I could see. "No one's coming for you," he said through gritted teeth. "You are nothing but a worthless, disgusting whore. No one will ever miss you."

"Bastian will miss me." I was going to die anyway, so I decided to go down like a man. I worked a mouthful of saliva onto my tongue and spit it in Jerome's face. He wiped the liquid from his cheek and stared at me with such hatred I thought his eyes would ignite into flames.

He raised his knife over his head, but before he plunged it into my chest, a loud bang came from downstairs, immediately followed by the sound of rapid gunfire. An evil grin crossed Jerome's lips. "Sounds like your boyfriend made it after all. I'm glad my men are giving him a nice welcome."

My heart sank, shredding to pieces. This was everything I was trying to avoid. Bastian *did* come for me, and now he was paying with his life. Dying by Jerome's hand was what I deserved for bringing such a wonderful man to his end. Maybe, if I was lucky, there would be life after this one, and Bastian and I would see each other again. The thought brought a peaceful smile to my lips. I was ready to die.

"What the fuck are you smiling about?" Jerome barked. Just as his knife descended toward my chest, the closed door behind him exploded into dust. Before Jerome could even turn around to see the cause, two large hands circled his body; hands I recognized as belonging to my love.

Bastian's fingers squeezed Jerome's chest until they actually sank inside his flesh. His digits wrapped around the curved bones of Jerome's rib cage, and pulled them apart as Bastian roared so loudly it shook the bed against the floorboards. Jerome's face contorted into a look of fear and anguish and the blade dropped from his hand. His bones popped and splintered as the skin of his chest stretched and split from his neck to his groin, spilling blood and organs onto the floor. Bastian dropped the ripped sack that was once Jerome to the ground and stomped his heart for good measure.

I was blown away by Bastian's power and raw strength, and now understood why he was not afraid of Jerome or any of his men. I breathed a deep sigh of relief that my lover was safe and the man who haunted my dreams was gone, but groaned at the answering pain that burned across my stomach.

Bastian's eyes rose from the bloody heap on the floor to me, and the anger etched onto his face melted into distress. "Cielito!" He stepped to the bed and gripped the ropes that bound my hands, ripping them apart in one pull before releasing my feet the same way. He tore my shirt from my body with one hand and gasped at the sight of the deep laceration across my trunk. "Oh Cielito, what has he done to you?"

"It's okay," I whispered. I tried to raise my hand to run it through his beautiful curls, but I was too weak from blood loss and exhaustion. "I'm just glad I got to see you one last time, and know that you're safe."

"No." He shook his head forcefully. "I won't lose you." He leaned down and pressed his tongue to the bottom of my wound. He licked a slow line along the gash, and my eyes widened at the sight of my skin immediately fusing together, forming a long, pale pink scar. Though I now wasn't losing any more blood, I'd still lost too much already.

Bastian lifted his wrist to his mouth and bit into the flesh with his elongated fangs. He then held the oozing wound to my lips. "Drink, Cielito; please. It will help you heal. Please, my love." My heart squeezed at the desperation in his voice. I nodded slightly and closed my lips around the puncture sites.

When I sucked a mouthful of his blood onto my tongue, I was shocked at its sweet flavor. It tasted like warm chocolate sauce; not at all the bitter, metallic flavor I was expecting. When I swallowed the thick liquid down my throat, my body warmed from the inside out. My headache ebbed away. My strength increased. I began greedily sucking down more of the healing liquid but stopped suddenly. I didn't want to hurt Bastian by taking too much; he'd be no better off than I was.

Bastian combed his fingers through my messy hair and smiled gently. "Drink, my love. You will not harm me." I swallowed several more mouthfuls until my stomach no longer ached and I felt better than I could ever remember. When I pulled my lips from his wrist, Bastian didn't fight me. He simply pressed his tongue to the wound and I watched in awe as the dripping holes closed up. It was a trick that could never get old. I rested my head back against the mattress and let my eyes slide closed, embracing the pleasant tingle that overtook my body.

Bastian kissed my cheek and whispered into my ear, "Open your eyes, Milo." When I did, I gasped at the soft golden light that surrounded us.

"What's happening?" *Are we dying? Are we dead? Is that why I'm not in pain anymore?*

"It is our bond," Bastian replied quietly, as if not to break the reverence of the moment. "By drinking from one another, we have claimed our soulmate and solidified the binding between us."

Suddenly, a strand of golden light protruded from Bastian's head, and was soon followed by one from mine. "Holy shit," I whispered. I raised my finger to touch the cord connected to my brow, but Bastian took my hand and gently shook his head no before I could make contact. "Sorry." My lover smiled and kissed my fingertip.

"This represents our mental link. We will be able to communicate with one another without words. I cannot read all of your thoughts; only the ones you want me to hear in my mind. The same goes for you, Cielito. No matter our distance from one another, we will always be connected." The two strands touched ends, forming into one, and grew brighter.

A second cord of light breached each of our stomachs. I didn't try to touch this one. "This represents the binding of our bodies. As mates, our life lines will mirror one another. You will inherit my immortality, but if killed, I too shall perish, for I would not want to live without you. If I am killed, your life will be cut short as well. You will also experience increased metabolism and strength. My blood will heal and strengthen you if you become injured or weak, and your blood will sustain my life force forever." Once again, the strands touched ends, connecting us together.

A third glittery cord appeared from both of our chests. "This indicates our spiritual link. I can feel your emotions, and calm your anxieties or sorrows. It is difficult to be away from you, as my soul always calls out to its other half, and aches when we are apart. You complete me in every way." The ends touched, and we were linked together by three golden ropes.

Suddenly, the ropes broke from our bodies. They weaved into a tight braid and each end entered our chests at the level of our hearts. The braid glowed brightly, and the golden light around us illuminated until it was nearly blinding. And then it was all gone. I looked to Bastian with concern, worried something went wrong. He only smiled brightly, his eyes glistening with moisture.

"Milo Walker, we are now eternally bonded through body, mind and spirit. I will love, desire, and protect you all the days of my life."

My eyes clouded with tears and I pulled Bastian into a tight hug. "Oh Papi, I love you so much. I'm so sorry I left; I was scared something would happen to you because of me. I didn't want you to get hurt. I thought the best way to keep you safe was to get out of your life and let you find another mate. I didn't want to leave you, I swear it. I only did it to help."

Bastians hands snaked beneath me and held me even tighter against him. "I was terrified. I thought I was going to lose you, Cielito. I understand why you left, but now I hope you see there is nothing to fear. I will protect you from everything that threatens you. You are my life, Milo. And please understand, even if we had not completed our bond, I could never have another mate, nor would I want one. I am fated to you. I can only drink from you. I can only become excited by you. I can and will only love and desire you for all time."

"Even if we hadn't bonded...you couldn't drink any other blood?" Bastian shook his head no. "And you die without blood?" He nodded. "Oh my god, Papi; I could have killed you! If I left...and you didn't find me..." I burst into tears. In my hopes to keep him safe, I nearly destroyed him.

"Shh, Milo, it's alright, my love." He scooped me into his arms and sat on the edge of the bed, cradling me against his chest. "No more thoughts on that. You are here in my arms now, just as you're supposed to be. We have each other, and that is how it shall always remain."

I sniffled and my tears dried up as Bastian pumped love and serenity into me. It was incredible to know he would always be there to look after me. I wished I could protect him the way he could protect me, or fill him with positive thoughts and feelings. Maybe I didn't have super strength or paranormal abilities, but there *was* something I could give to him.

"*Bastian*," I tried telling him with my mind. His hold loosened on me and he looked down into my eyes, letting me know it worked. *"I promise to love you as fully and fiercely as I can for all of my days. I will honor you, be faithful to you, be honest with you, and promise to never run from you again."*

"Thank you, my love. That is everything I've ever longed to hear." He leaned in to give me a long, slow kiss.

"Damn, guys," sounded from the shattered doorway. Bastian and I separated and turned to find a blood-covered Sam grinning widely at us. "There's a mutilated body like ten inches from you and you're sucking face?"

"Do you really feel you're the right person to judge the appropriateness of displays of affection?" Dante asked as he stepped into the room behind Sam.

"I'm not judging; I'm applauding. That's hot as fuck right there."

Dante sighed and shook his head at Sam before looking to us. "The bottom floor is secure. The threat has been neutralized."

"Everyone is dead?" I asked breathlessly. Dante and Sam both nodded. I sprung from Bastian's arms and ran across the room, grabbing up my friends into a big hug. "Thank you so much! You all saved me! I don't know what I would have done if not for you! I…" My breath caught. "Where's Ben? Oh god, is he okay?"

Dante released me and gave a small smile. "Thank you for your concern, but he is fine. He is waiting for us in the car outside. Although I do believe I've been away from him for far too long. Shall we return home?"

"Yes," I answered readily. I turned to Bastian, who was now at my side. "Let's go home."

Bastian squeezed me in a side-hug. "I want nothing more, Cielito. Besides, we need to start planning our ceremony." He turned to our friends. "We've bonded."

Sam smiled, gave me another quick embrace, and slapped Bastian on the shoulder. "Congrats."

"Yes, many congratulations," Dante offered with a bow of his head. It felt weird to be having this conversation next to a dead guy while everyone was dripping with spilled blood. "Now, let us leave before the authorities arrive. Though we are not close to neighbors, I'm afraid our noise may still attract them soon." We all nodded and quickly left the room, with Bastian gripping my hand in his.

I gasped when we reached the bottom floor; bullets riddled the ground, body parts were dismembered and strewn across the floorboards, and blood soaked nearly every surface.

"We're messy, but effective," Sam shrugged.

"And I couldn't be more grateful," I told him seriously. He smiled and we hurried out of the house.

I spotted Bastian's SUV across the street, along with two big blue eyes peeking out of the back window. Once he saw that we were out and alone, Ben leapt out of the vehicle and ran to us at top speed, carrying a half empty bottle of tequila and an old t-shirt over his shoulder.

"Milo!" He wrapped me in a fierce hug with his free arm. "I'm so glad you're okay!" He kissed my cheek and then released me from his hold and gasped when he saw the long, fresh scar across my abdomen. "Oh, Milo," he whispered sadly. "I'm so sorry."

"It's okay," I answered honestly. "It means I survived, right?" Ben nodded vigorously and Bastian kissed the top of my head.

Ben sighed as he looked at the rest of our group. "I'm just so glad *all* of you are okay!" He gave Sam and Bastian hugs and cheek kisses as well, and to my surprise, didn't even flinch when he touched the copious amount of blood that covered them. He must have been too relieved to be leery. Ben then pulled his husband down to his level for a lengthy kiss and tight embrace.

"What are you doing with that bottle?" Bastian asked, interrupting the lovers.

"I found this in your trunk and I want to help," Ben answered firmly before looking between all of us, pulling the shirt from his shoulder and a lighter from his pocket. "Can I?"

Bastian's lips curled into a wicked grin. "Torch it." Ben squealed and did a little happy dance.

"Forget everything I said," Sam said with wide eyes and an even wider grin. "You're fucking terrifying, babe."

"Thanks!" Ben replied before giggling and running toward the house. The little sweetie also had a dark side and I liked it a *lot*.

"Be careful, Amado!" Dante called as he jogged after his husband. Only a few minutes later, the house was engulfed in hot orange flames from Ben's handmade bottle bomb. Hopefully when the police did find the scene, they'd chalk it up to gang violence. Regardless, all of my fears, nightmares, oppression and bad memories were being reduced to ash.

"Come," Dante announced as he and Ben rejoined our group. "Let's go home. We have much to celebrate."

"Fuck yeah!" Sam cried, punching the air. "Everybody's gonna get laid!"

Chapter Eleven

Bastian

Milo moaned as I massaged the shampoo into his hair. I'd already triple bagged all of our clothing from the night and discarded them, anxious to get rid of the acrid stench of Jerome's blood. Then I ushered my beloved into the shower to scrub the offending smell from his skin, as well as soothe his nerves and muscles beneath the jets.

I pressed my fingers firmly into his scalp and circled them, cleansing his hair and kneading his flesh. I'd already washed his hair once, along with his body, but I knew how much he enjoyed this; almost as much as I enjoyed doing it for him. Milo's eyes were closed and a look of total bliss and relaxation took over his features. I shielded his brow with one hand while tipping his head back into the stream with the other. I combed through his locks to rinse away all of the suds, making sure to not get anything in his eyes. When his hair was clean, I took advantage of his closed eyes and upturned face and pressed my lips to his. His mouth twitched against mine as it folded into a smile.

"This is incredible," he whispered against my lips. "Being back here with you in our home." My heart nearly burst; until tonight, Milo had always referred to this place as mine; my apartment, my bed, my theater...but it seemed after our bonding and being free from Jerome's powerful hold, he understood that he belonged here as well. What was mine was his; *ours*, forever.

"*And* it's incredible that everything that hurt me and terrified me has been erased in one single night." Milo gave me a sad smile and shook his head. "I wish I would have told you where they lived the very first night you found me."

"Me too, Cielito," I admitted, pushing his wet hair behind his ear. "But they are gone now, and you are safe. No one shall ever harm you again, because I will not let them." My eyes trailed down his body to the new scar that spread across his abdomen. I touched it gingerly with my fingertips and my heart ached. "I'm just so sorry I didn't get to you in time to keep you from such pain."

"This isn't your fault," he replied firmly. He took my hand and squeezed until I looked into his eyes. "It's mine; I never should have left you."

"The fault lies only with Jerome and those other evil men," I insisted. "You felt you *had* to leave because of the fear they instilled in you. You never deserved this; you only deserve the best things in life, and I plan to give you all of them and so much more."

"Thank you, Papi," Milo replied with glassy eyes. "But I have everything I need right here." He squeezed my hand again, pulling me down to him until our lips touched. When we parted, Milo trapped his lip between his teeth and chewed on it as his guilt permeated the steamy air around us.

"What is it, Cielito?"

"Well...I thought of something I kinda want, but I feel like a douche for asking. Especially after what I just said. It's nothing I *need*, but-"

"Tell me and you shall have it," I promised. I wanted to make his every dream come true and shower him with every gift he desired.

"The other day..." he started, before dropping his gaze to the floor. I'd found it was something he did when feeling guilty, unsure or unconfident. I interrupted him by touching my finger to his chin and gently pressing up until he lifted his head.

"Milo, always hold your head up with pride," I begged. "You are brave, strong and true, and have no reason to ever doubt yourself. Besides that, I cannot get enough of these gorgeous eyes. When you look at me, I am blessed."

"Damn." Milo blinked his eyes hard and I smiled. I loved when he was so touched by my feelings for him that he wasn't sure what to say.

"So please, my love, look at me and tell me what it is you desire."

"Well, the other day you mentioned you would pay for me to get a tattoo that would cover this one." He pointed to the offensive word on his wrist. "I would really like that. I wanted it as soon as you mentioned it, but I guess I was scared. I was convinced Jerome would find me and I thought if he saw I'd covered up what he did, it would be worse for me somehow." He narrowed his eyes. "That sounds stupid, doesn't it?"

"Milo, nothing you feel or believe is stupid," I assured. "I understand your previous concerns." He breathed a heavy sigh of relief and graced me with a pretty smile. "But I am happy to provide you with that, Cielito. In the morning, we will research the best tattoo artists in the area. When you find the one you wish to work with, we'll make an appointment for them to help you create a design you love."

"Thank you, Papi." He blinked his eyes again to stave off tears. "Would it be too much to ask to cover this one too?" As he asked the silly question, he touched his fingers to his newest scar.

"Nothing is too much for you," I told him seriously. "I want to give you the world, but it would still not be enough." Milo lost his fight with his tears as one slipped down his cheek. "I love every inch of your body just as it is, but I want you to love your skin as much as I do. It would honor me to provide you with this."

"Thank you," he whispered once more. "Do you think you could help me with one more thing?" As he asked, his eyes drifted downward, but he caught himself and snapped them back up to my gaze, which warmed me to my core.

"Anything."

"Could you help me make an appointment downstairs? At the clinic?" He nervously twisted his fingers in front of him, but kept his eyes on me. "I was going to ask Ben, but I want you to go with me. I want to make sure I'm healthy. I mean, if I'm gonna last forever, that's probably important, right? Plus, I want to be with you fully; I want to drink your seed to make it a part of me. I want to explode inside you and feel you inside me too. I need to make sure I won't harm you. I won't do anything that will mess with your crazy long lifespan."

I couldn't stop my body from reacting to the deliciously naughty things he was describing; my cock slowly rose until it was tall and firm, and my mind was fuzzy with lust. I needed to focus, however, and explain things to Milo. I shook the fog from my mind and cupped my lover's cheeks.

"Oh Cielito, I'm sorry I haven't been clear enough." I'd never had to explain vampire culture to a human before, and I was afraid I'd done a terrible job. Perhaps if I'd been more clear with Milo when I told him I *was* a vampire, he never would have left thinking it was in my best interest. It was something I'd never forgive myself for, but I was determined to do better from here on out. "Remember when I said I could be killed by being beheaded or having my heart pierced or removed?" He nodded. "That's *all* that can kill me. Jerome's men shot me dozens of times, but their bullets had no ill effects on my body."

"Jesus!" Milo's face paled and he rocked backward on his heels.

Damn. That was still terrible. "Please don't think on it, Milo. Like I said, I'm fine. My point is, I am immune to human diseases. I cannot be affected by them or harbor them. As my mate, neither can you. You are impervious to illness. Nothing besides an outside force can harm or kill you."

"And if I had a disease before we mated?" he asked worriedly.

"It's gone."

"Holy shit," he exclaimed with wide eyes. "So not only am I going to live forever, I'll never get sick? Like, not even a cold?" I nodded. "Damn, if more humans knew about this, they'd be jealous as fuck." His speech sometimes reminded me of the way Sam spoke, except that it wasn't irritating; it was adorable coming from my perfect lover. Milo began chuckling, and I cocked my head.

"What's so funny, Cielito?"

"Nothing, it's just..." he laughed some more. "Well, I guess that explains the condoms."

"I don't understand. Was something wrong with them?"

That only made my sweet man laugh harder until he abruptly stopped. "Wait...does that mean...am I the first person you've been with?"

My heart sank. I cupped his cheeks in my hands and hoped I didn't hurt his feelings when I answered, "I wish I could answer yes, but I cannot lie to you. I'm so sorry I did not have the willpower to wait for you, my fated mate. I wish I could take back every previous encounter of my life. I hope you can forgive me."

"Hey, hey, it's okay," he said quickly, putting his hands over mine. "I didn't mean that; three hundred twenty eight years is a long fucking time to hold out." He gave me a lopsided smile and I was glad to feel no ill will coming off of him. "I meant am I the first *human* you've been with."

Ohhh. "You are." Waves of Milo's love and lust nearly knocked me over. I was happy that my words pleased him. "And please believe me when I say I've had no feelings for anyone in my past. You are the first person to steal my heart, and the first and only one I will ever love. When *we* make love together, it isn't just a physical release. It is a burning desire to bring you pleasure and feel you in and around me. It is a strengthening and sharing of our emotional and spiritual bonds. It is everything, Milo."

I blinked in surprise as Milo dropped to his knees before me, splashing in the shallow puddle at the bottom of the shower. He wrapped his lips around the crown of my dick and I had to steady myself with a hand to the wall to keep from falling over.

"I love you so damn much, Bastian," Milo spoke into my mind as his tongue circled around my slit, lapping up every drop that leaked out of me. *"You are the first and only man I'll ever love, too. You showed me what life could be, and made mine worth living. I want to make you feel as good as you make me feel every second of every day."* I decided this was the sexiest and best way to share a mental link.

Milo sucked hard around my tip as his fist circled my shaft. He stroked me quickly as his tongue flicked against my sensitive flesh. *"I want to taste you, Papi. I want you to burst in my mouth and I'm going to drink down every drop."*

"Ohh god..." Milo's sexy words made me dizzy with want and lust. I cradled my head back onto my shoulders and relished the feel of his skin on mine. He jacked my cock in a corkscrew motion, pulling a steady stream of pre-cum from me, which he greedily sucked down.

He gripped my balls in his free hand and tugged them down gently as his other hand stroked me and his tongue laved my tip. There was only one thing I could think of to make this moment more perfect.

"I want to taste you too, Cielito," I begged. Milo's ministrations stopped, and he looked up at me in question. His eyes were wide and lust-blown and his plush lips were stretched around my girth. He was so beautiful I nearly came at the sight.

Milo pulled his mouth back slowly and released my cock with a *pop*. "How?"

"Stand up and I'll show you," I replied in a husky tone. My lover jumped quickly to his feet. I lifted him from the shower floor and he instinctively wrapped his legs around my waist, though he still appeared confused. I peeled him from my body and easily turned him upside down in my arms so that his face was level with my firm, dripping cock. Since he was quite a bit shorter than me, I would need to bow my head to reach his. Milo's hands gripped my thighs and I worried that this was too much for him. "Is this okay, Cielito? Are you frightened you'll fall?" Our bodies *were* slick from the water cascading around us.

"No, Papi; I trust you with my life. I know you'd never drop me." I shivered when his warm breath hit my wet skin. "This isn't from fear; it's for leverage." With that, he took my crown between his lips and pulled against the back of my thighs, swallowing over half of my length down his throat. It took all of my focus to keep my knees from buckling.

Milo's legs were spread with his shins resting on my shoulders, and his fuzzy sack and pretty pink pucker were staring back at me. I brushed my tongue across his testicles and he moaned around my cock. I took one of his sensitive orbs into my mouth and worshipped its surface with my tongue. I flicked against it as I sucked gently, popping it in and out of my mouth.

"Oh my god, Bastian, that feels amazing!"

At Milo's silent approval, I widened my mouth and sucked both of his balls into it. I swallowed around them, bouncing them against each other, my tongue, and my cheeks. Milo's hand shot off of my leg onto the wall, knocking over a bottle of shampoo. I swished my cheeks, suckling and licking his sensitive skin as his fingers clawed at the wall. *If he likes that, I have something even better for him*.

I dropped his testicles from my mouth, drawing a whimper of protest from my lover as he bobbed his head up and down my length. I only smiled, and pressed my tongue to his pucker, lapping across his wrinkled flesh.

"Holy fucking shit!" echoed off the shower walls as Milo released my cock from his lips.

"*You like this?*" I asked as I feverishly licked his hole.

"I've never felt anything like it. Please, Papi; more!"

I flattened my tongue on his pucker and thrashed my head back and forth, covering my taste buds with his sweet, musky flavor and flicking water drops in every direction as they showered over him. Milo knocked over two more bottles as his hands desperately searched for purchase. He finally settled on gripping my thighs once more, and taking in more of my length than ever before down his throat.

He sucked hard, quickly bobbing his head as I feasted on his asshole. When I slid the tip of my tongue inside him, however, Milo dropped my cock once more to scream out in bliss. I wriggled my slick appendage, sinking it further inside him and licking against his internal walls as my lover keened and whimpered the most beautiful sounds. Milo's legs trembled against my shoulders and his chest heaved on my pelvis. He wrapped his lips around the tip of my cock, but seemed too blissed out to move.

I gave an experimental roll of my hips, gently sinking several inches of my aching cock into his mouth. *"Is this okay?"* I would do nothing my mate didn't enjoy.

"Yes, Papi. *You're making me feel too good to move. Fuck my mouth while you eat my ass!"*

That seemed pretty definite. I closed my lips around his tight hole and sucked as I pistoned my hips back and forth. Milo hummed, allowing me to slide further down his throat, though I was careful not to be too rough or go too deep. I licked, nibbled, sucked and ate his tasty hole until his entire body shook.

"Bastian, I'm getting close. It feels too good, Papi; I'm gonna blow."

I wanted to eat his ass until he exploded all over my chest, but I also wanted my first taste of his seed. I reluctantly pulled my tongue from his hole as Milo's body quaked. I turned my head to the side to capture his firm cock between my lips. His length was coated in pre-cum, allowing him to slide easily to the back of my throat. I swallowed and flexed my throat muscles around him, milking the flesh of his cock.

"*Suck me! Please, suck me, Papi!*" I gave him everything I had, sucking him hard and bobbing my head along his length as I rocked my hips, burying myself in the tight heat of his throat. Milo's fingers sank into the flesh of my thighs, cutting tiny crescents into my skin, which regrettably healed instantly. "*Bastian! Ohhh god!*"

Milo's cock swelled and erupted in my mouth, coating my tongue in his salty sweet release. I savored the flavor on my taste buds before swallowing the thick liquid down my eager throat. He trembled, moaned, and grappled at my legs as he continued to throb between my lips.

Finally tasting my lover brought me right up to the edge. I growled low as I rocked my hips and Milo swished and swirled his tongue against my sensitive tip. My pelvis burned with delight and my balls lifted to my body. I tightened my grip around Milo and screamed his name as I exploded. I pulsed burst after burst of seed into my lover's throat, and he swallowed greedily, moaning at the flavor. He pulled and milked me with his lips until my legs trembled.

I carefully maneuvered Milo until he was face to face with me. Instead of standing on his shaky legs, he wrapped them around my waist again. He settled his cheek against my chest, and I kissed his wet hair before whispering in his ear, "You are delicious, my love."

"You too, Papi," he whispered back. Sweet Milo was sated, content, and sleepy. I cuddled him against me, allowing the jets to cascade over his back in their soothing pattern, and held him until the water began to run cold.

I twisted the knobs and stepped out of the shower, grabbing a fluffy towel from the rack. I patted us dry the best I could without setting Milo down on the floor. We weren't perfectly dry, but I didn't care. I needed to hold him. I needed him close. After the night we had, I didn't want to let him out of my arms for even a moment, and the way Milo clung to me told me he felt the same way. We needed the comfort and assurance that we were here together, and that everything was okay.

I carried him to our bed and lay him down gently. I climbed in beside him and Milo was quick to wrap an arm and leg around my body and lay his head on my shoulder.

"You know, when I left, what broke my heart the most was thinking you'd never hold me again," Milo admitted quietly. "When I'm in your arms, I feel so safe and protected and loved."

"You are all of those things and more," I promised. I pulled him closer to me and dropped a kiss on his head, thinking about Fate's pairing. We truly were perfect together. My sweet Milo needed a safe haven; a person whom he could trust with his heart and body. He'd never had a home where he felt safe or loved. And I wanted someone to give me purpose; someone special I could love and protect. I craved someone I could dote on and share my wealth with; someone who needed me as much as I needed them. And I desperately needed Milo.

My beloved breathed a giant yawn and snuggled deeper into my side, nuzzling his smooth cheek over my chest. His body and mind were exhausted. It filled me with pride to know I was the safe place where he could lay his head; the person he trusted to look over him while he rested.

"No harm will ever come to you again, my sweet little sky," I whispered into the silent air.

Milo hummed and kissed my chest. "I love you, Bastian. For all of forever."

A grin crossed my lips at my man's perfect promise. "I love you too, Milo. For all of eternity." Within moments, his breaths became deep and slow, and he was gone to the world. I hoped with everything I was that he would finally have sweet dreams.

Chapter Twelve

Milo

"May I?" Ben asked, holding up my leather bracelet. My friend was in my apartment, helping me get ready for Bastian's and my bonding ceremony. We'd been together for two weeks, which in human time seemed crazy to basically be getting married, but everyone here acted like two weeks was a crazy *long* time to have waited. I was still getting used to some of the culture, but in all honesty, I would have married Bastian the night he saved me from Jerome.

Of course, we weren't *technically* getting married. He asked me if a legal wedding ceremony was something I wanted, and that he would make it happen if it was, but I couldn't care less. We were going to be together forever, and titles didn't matter much to me. I *did*, however, legally change my last name to Santos. I had no happy memories or special meaning attached to my previous last name, and seeing how thrilled it made Bastian for me to take his name, it was worth it.

"Thanks, Ben." I held out my hand for him to tie the straps around my wrist, but it was the opposite hand than where I normally wore it. I didn't want to cover up my other wrist anymore; it now held a beautiful floral tattoo that completely hid the old one Jerome gave me in his kitchen. I also surprised Bastian by having the tattoo artist permanently write my lover's name above the design. My big man loved it, but said he never wanted me to think he held any ownership or priority over me, which is why 'Milo' was now scripted across his wrist as well.

The scar on my abdomen was also covered by new ink; an awesome swirly tribal design. All of the physical reminders of my past were long gone. Sure, there were still painful memories that hung around, but for every bad one I could think of, Bastian had already given me a dozen good ones. Including the ones of him getting me off by just licking the silver bars that now passed through my nipples.

"There," Ben smiled, looking me up and down. "You look very handsome."

I was dressed in my nicest pair of black jeans and a slate gray dress shirt, along with my boots of course; I only ever took them off to shower or sleep. When I first chose the outfit, I was worried it wasn't dressy enough; I didn't want to appear disrespectful to such a solemn event in the vampire world. However, Bastian said he only cared about my comfort and happiness. He said if I'd rather wear pajama pants and a t-shirt for our ceremony, he'd be totally fine with that; that it was my day. But it was

Bastian's day, too, which is why I chose the dress shirt. It wouldn't have been my first pick, but I wanted to look nice for him.

"Hey hey!" Sam called as he entered the apartment. Ben and I were in the bedroom, but could hear him just fine. "Is anybody naked?"

Ben giggled. "No, come on in; we're dressed!"

"Dammit!" Sam replied as he entered the room with a wide smile on his face. I'd grown closer to both men, and had come to love Sam's playful sense of humor. I could tell it was a little much for Bastian to handle sometimes, and Dante looked like he wanted to throttle him more often than not, but I loved the guy; Ben too. They were my best friends in the whole world. "Hey there good lookin'!"

"Hey," Ben and I both answered, making Sam laugh.

"You're not wrong; you both look hot." Sam gave me a quick one-armed hug before kissing Ben's cheek. Ben and Sam were both dressed to the nines in black tuxes, which only made me more self conscious about what I was wearing. "Look what I've got!" Sam produced a box from behind his back.

"Sam, you didn't have to get me anything!" I insisted.

"I didn't," he shrugged. "This is from your man. He asked me to bring it down to you." Bastian was upstairs with Dante as he prepared for our ceremony. "Now I feel like an asshole for *not* getting you something, though."

"Sam, you helped save my life a couple of weeks ago," I reminded him. "I wouldn't be here if it weren't for you, so you most definitely *did* get me something."

"Oh yeah," he grinned. "Well then, you're welcome."

Ben scoffed and slapped his friend's shoulder, but I just laughed. "Let's see what this is, shall we?"

"What if it's something naughty?" Ben whispered. "Should we step out of the room?"

"Hell no! I'm standing in line to try it out," Sam countered, making me laugh again.

I pulled the red silk ribbon off of the box and opened the lid to reveal a long black trench coat. I gasped and lifted the garment from the package, running my fingers over the soft fabric. The lapels and cuffs were made of supple leather which was embossed with an intricate scroll design. The same pattern was on the silver buttons that ran down the front. "It's gorgeous," I whispered in a trembling voice.

"Aw, that's the sweetest thing ever!" Ben gushed, clapping his hands in front of him. "Try it on!"

I pushed my arms through the sleeves and clasped the buttons. The material was buttery soft and felt like heaven. "What do you think?"

"I think you're gonna knock his socks off," Sam answered with a smile. I grinned at the touching, so-unlike-Sam sentiment. "And send his dick rocketing off his body." *Ah, there he is.*

Ben shook his head at his friend and turned his smirk to me. "He means you look beautiful." He leaned in and kissed my cheek. "Are you ready to get...um...bonded?" Sam snorted and I grinned widely. Since this wasn't technically a wedding like Ben and Dante had, I wasn't sure of the term either, but Ben's sweetness did me in every damn time.

I took a deep breath and nodded determinedly. "I'm ready."

*****

Bastian

"Have a drink, amigo," Dante offered as he poured me a large glass of wine. "It will help settle your nerves." I took the glass with a bow of my head.

"Thank you, but my nerves are calm. It is my heart that is racing."

Dante's smile brightened. "You are truly in love, my friend." He patted my shoulder and sat next to me on his sofa as I drained my glass. "I cannot begin to tell you how happy I am that you have found your mate. You have served beside me all of our lives as my most loyal and trusted friend. You deserve this more than anyone."

"Thank you, sir." Dante's head cocked and he gave me a warm smile. "Thank you, Dante."

"You're most welcome. Now, in honor of your blessed bond, I got you a little gift." He reached into the breast pocket of his tux and pulled out a small square box.

"Dante, you shouldn't have-"

"I insist," he interrupted. "Trust me, you'll like it." He winked and I took the box from his hand. When I opened it, I found a police badge, whose shiny surface was speckled with blood.

"I'm not sure I understand."

Dante's grin gleamed wickedly. "It belonged to the officer who betrayed your mate. He was not only tied up with Jerome; he was involved in many other nefarious activities." He patted my knee. "Not to worry; he had no family and the official report will claim brake line failure of his vehicle and a tall cliffside."

I didn't know what to say. I was deeply touched that my friend - my prince -

cared so much about me and my mate that he personally cut the last loose thread that could potentially cause Milo harm.

"I-" my voice cracked and I cleared my throat. I looked into his eyes with all of the sincerity and gratitude I could muster. "Thank you, Dante."

He pulled me into a tight embrace. "Of course. I wish you and your beloved nothing but an eternity of happiness." He patted my back and stood up. "Speaking of which, I believe we have a ceremony to get to."

*****

Milo

"We'll be in the front row," Ben promised with a final squeeze of my hand. He and Sam had walked me down to the nightclub where our ceremony was taking place. Now they were waiting with me right outside the door where I'd be entering the club from the side.

"Thank you." I hugged Ben and then Sam.

"Knock 'em dead," my other friend said with a wink once I released him. "And just remember; if you get horny when you see your man, we'll all be able to smell it."

"Dammit, Sam! Now I'm gonna be all self conscious," I scolded, though there was no heat behind it. I didn't care if everyone knew how my big man affected me. Hell, we were bonded soulmates; that's how we were *supposed* to affect each other.

"*I* won't be able to smell it," Ben offered, trying to make me feel better.

"He'll just be able to see your boner," Sam shrugged, and Ben slapped him on the shoulder, making him laugh.

"I love you guys," I told them seriously. I couldn't imagine my life without these sweet, crazy men at my side.

"Aw, we love you too," Ben gushed with a wide smile.

"Ditto," Sam winked. They each gave me a quick kiss on the cheek and stepped toward the door. Before Sam went through, he turned around and made a wafting motion in front of his face. I flipped him off, making him laugh loudly before he followed Ben, slipping inside the club to take their seats.

Several long minutes passed as I waited to hear Dante's cue from the other side of the door. As Coven Master, it was his responsibility to oversee the ceremony, but he told Bastian and me that as our friend, it was his honor and pleasure.

"Welcome everyone," Dante's voice rang out. "We are gathered here today to celebrate a most joyous occasion; the bonding between a vampire and his soulmate. I ask that everyone stand to honor Bastian Santos and Milo Santos as they enter."

There's my cue. I took a deep breath and opened the door with shaking hands. When I stepped inside the club, my heart sped at the sight of hundreds, if not a thousand or more, vampires standing to honor Bastian and me as we entered. All of them were smiling or bowing their heads with respect when I looked at them. My eyes stung; never before had I felt such happiness or pride. These people had accepted me into their company with open arms and judgement-free minds. I'd received dozens of well wishes over the past couple of weeks from vampires welcoming me to the coven. Because of Bastian, I now had a partner for life, best friends, and a loving home.

I pulled my eyes from the crowd to the opposite side of the room, where Bastian entered and was walking toward me. I couldn't stop a few tears from sliding down my cheeks as I saw him; his posture and expression were exuding love and pride and happiness and it took my breath away.

"*You look gorgeous,*" I told him through our link. I'd never seen him look *more* gorgeous; I was expecting him to be wearing a tux like our friends and the rest of the males in the room, but he was dressed in a long leather trench coat that matched mine. His curls were shiny and soft as they fell over his shoulders, and his cinnamon eyes glimmered in the low lighting.

"*And you are stunning, my love. I am surely the envy of every unbonded man and woman in this room.*"

I couldn't stop the dumb, cheesy grin that spread over my face at his words. No one had ever looked at me as anything other than a cheap thrill, but Bastian saw me as the most precious and desired man on the planet. *"Thank you so much for the coat, Papi; I love it,"* I told him when I realized I still hadn't thanked him for the gift.

"You are most welcome, though as I see it on you now, I believe it was more of a gift for myself. You are a vision of beauty."

"Damn."

Bastian chuckled softly as we reached each other and he took both of my hands in his. He lowered his head to kiss the backs of my knuckles, and we turned our attention to Dante, who looked puffed up with pride and glee.

"You may be seated," he began, and all of the crowd sat swiftly and silently. I'd never get over the natural grace vampires held. "Before we begin, I would like to address the couple." He took his eyes from the congregation to look at the two of us with a gentle smile. "Bastian, it is my deepest honor to be standing here today. You have served me well for over three hundred years, both as my most loyal subject and my dearest friend. You have saved my life countless times, protected my body and my honor, and stood by me in my darkest hours. You are a remarkable man."

"Thank you, sir," Bastian replied with a dip of his head. I heard quiet sniffling coming from the crowd, and turned to see Ben sobbing into Sam's chest as his friend rubbed soothing circles on his back. Sam rolled his eyes playfully at me before kissing Ben's head. I smiled at the pair and turned back to face Dante. His expression was flashing between lovestruck over his sweet husband and fury over someone besides him caring for his lover. He shook his head and looked to me.

"Milo, you put your own life in danger when you thought it would keep your mate and your friends safe. That kind of sacrifice deserves the utmost respect. It is in times of crisis that a person's true colors are shown, and you have proven yourself to be a remarkable man as well."

"Thank you, sir," I answered and bowed my head as Bastian had. My lover squeezed my hands in approval.

"I must also thank *you*," Dante continued. I looked at him in confusion, and he smiled. "You have brought my friend such joy and purpose. I have never seen him as happy and fulfilled as when he is in your presence." My lip trembled as I looked to Bastian, who winked in agreement. A shaky smile crossed my lips, and Ben's sobbing grew louder, garnering a few chuckles from the crowd.

"Milo, as you are now bonded to Bastian for eternity, you are invited to become a member of this coven if you so choose. Do you agree to abide by our rules, honor our members and protect your coven, mate and friends with your life?"

Bastian explained this to me nearly two weeks ago; as his mate, I would be welcomed into the coven, but had to promise to treat each member with respect and offer my allegiance to the prince. If I refused, I would still be bonded to Bastian, but unwelcome in this coven. He and I would have to move to another group, and be forever shamed and prohibited from coming back here. I had zero reservations; of course I would protect my mate and my friends (although I was sure they'd be the ones who could protect me better), and Dante had proven himself time and time again to be worthy of my allegiance. Not only by how he treats Bastian and Ben, but having saved my life when he gained nothing from it.

"I do," I announced firmly. "I am honored to become a member of this coven and swear to honor and protect its members.

I give my allegiance to you, Prince Dante Javier, and my loyalty and love to Bastian Santos."

Cheers erupted throughout the crowd at my words, and Bastian looked so proud I thought he might explode. Dante reached out to squeeze my shoulder and gave me a blinding smile.

"Milo, you are now officially a member of this coven, and will be forever surrounded by friends and kin." More applause sounded until Dante raised his hand, and everyone fell quiet. "I ask that each of you now present your mate with the token you have chosen to represent your bonding."

When Bastian explained this part of the ceremony to me last week, he said it was sort of like exchanging rings at a wedding; the couple chose something meaningful to them to either wear or display as a symbol of their bond. I immediately had a thought, but was afraid it was a little too 'out there'. However, Bastian loved the idea.

    He withdrew a vial from his pocket that contained a small amount of his blood mixed with an anticoagulant so that it wouldn't clot. The vial was attached to an ornate fixture and hung from a silver chain. I had a matching one in my pocket full of my own blood. The original idea was to collect the fluid at the ceremony, but every time Bastian fed from me, it ended in screaming, thrashing, cum-splattering ecstasy, and I didn't think the coven needed to see that. Even though he would have only bitten into my skin and extracted a few drops, I didn't want to take the chance.

    So, we ended up collecting the samples at home, and god *damn*, did we have fun doing it. I even bit Bastian's neck in a fit of passion, and was ecstatic to see the bonding scar that formed on his skin. My big man was ecstatic too; we both cried as we held each other, and then made passionate love all over again.

"Milo, I offer this to you as a symbol of our bond," Bastian announced as he fastened the necklace around my throat. "May you always remember you are the blood in my veins, the pulse in my chest, and the air in my lungs."

Suddenly, Ben wasn't the only one crying. Several members of the congregation were sniffling, and tears stained my cheeks as well. I wiped them away and steadied my breathing, not wanting to stutter through my presentation to Bastian.

I took the vial from my pocket. "Bastian, I offer this to you as a symbol of our bond." I fastened the chain around his neck. "Before we met, my life was a series of terrible and painful events. So many times, I just wanted it all to end." The sobs from the crowd grew stronger, making my heart swell; these people cared about me. "And then I met you, and found there was a reason for holding on. You showed me kindness and compassion and more love than I could ever imagine. You are not only my reason for living, but my very life. Please take this blood knowing you are just as integral to my existence as it is."

Bastian cupped both of my cheeks in his large hands and bent to rest his forehead on mine. He pushed his emotions into me, letting me feel the magnitude of the love he held for me. It made my breath hitch and drew more tears from my eyes.

"And every day I'll love you more," he promised. I crashed against his chest and wrapped my arms around his thick waist. He held me close and rocked me back and forth as I wept. It was the most beautiful moment of my life, and I didn't care that the entire coven was watching; I *wanted* them to share in our happiness.

Dante gently cleared his throat, and we managed to peel ourselves away from each other. "And so, by the power vested in me as Coven Master and Vampire Prince, I now announce these two to be bonded eternally; not only in the eyes of Fate and to each other, but in front of the coven of their peers. I offer my greatest blessings to this union. Bastian, please salute your beloved soulmate with a kiss."

Bastian wasted no time in cupping my cheeks again and pressing his lips to mine. The crowd erupted in cheers and whistles as we kissed and nibbled each other's lips. Tears slicked our flesh, but we didn't stop. I welcomed the salty flavor on my tongue as it slid against my lover's.

A weight slammed into my side, and I reluctantly pulled my lips from Bastian to look over and find Ben plastered against the two of us. "Congratulations, guys! I'm so happy for you!"

"Damn, give them some breathing room, babe," Sam insisted as he removed his friend from our sides. "Or at least dick room; you know they're hard after a kiss like that." Bastian growled at him, but I just snorted a laugh. I *was* hard, and could feel Bastian's length pressing into my stomach.

Dante took his husband in his arms. "Are you okay, Benny? I heard you crying in the audience."

"I'm okay, osito. I'm just so happy for our friends." They dissolved into kisses and cuddles. Sam looked between them and Bastian and me, who were still embracing one another, and instead of his typical eye roll, he gave a genuine smile.

I looked out at the rest of the club and noticed everyone else was gone, and the seats they had been sitting in were all folded and back in storage. It'd take a while to get used to vampire speed. The ceremony had been wonderful, but the way everyone just disappeared seemed like kind of a lackluster ending to it all.

"So...is it over?" I asked.

"Hell no," Sam replied, his grin growing wider. "Everybody just went to change for the party. Nobody can get their freak on in a tux."

"Party?"

Bastian tightened his hold on me. "I planned a celebration; it is my gift to you."

"Oh, Papi." I kissed his cheeks and lips in excitement, making him chuckle.

"Ooh, can we tell them about *our* gift?" Ben pleaded to his husband, who beamed and nodded. Ben came up to us again and took one of each of our hands. "Tay and I are going to Spain next week. We're visiting his parents and will be introduced to the kingdom. We want you to come with us! It's our treat and it'll be like a honeymoon for you guys! What do you say?"

He looked at us with such hope and anxiousness, like we were the ones who would be granting him a favor by going on this awesome free trip.

"That's amazing, Ben!" I wrapped him in a tight hug. "Thank you so much! I've never even been out of the *state* before!"

"Me neither!" he squealed. "Wait...no, Tay took me to Michigan a few weeks ago." A goofy smile crossed his lips and his eyes went unfocused as he thought about the trip, which was apparently pretty great. Sam snorted and Ben snapped back to himself. "Sorry. But yay! This is so exciting!"

Bastian laughed and held his hand out for Dante to shake. "Thank you, amigo; it will be wonderful to see our homeland again. Not to mention my parents."

"Oh god, I'll be meeting the in-laws!" My face paled; I hadn't thought about that.

Bastian was quick to wrap me up again. "They will love you, Cielito. I can promise you that." He kissed my cheek and pushed a wave of love and support into me, calming my nerves. He looked to Dante. "But who will look after the coven while we are gone?" Being Dante's Second, the responsibility would normally fall to him.

"Don't worry, I got this," Sam said, puffing his chest out.

"You certainly do not," Dante replied, rubbing his temples. Sam's jaw dropped in offense, but Dante ignored him. "I've asked Dmitri to look after things, and he has graciously accepted. We've had no threats against us since both Hugo and Jerome's groups have been eradicated, and we will only be gone two weeks, so I don't foresee any issues arising."

"I could have handled it," Sam pouted, kicking the ground.

"I know you could have," Ben assured, hugging his friend. "But I want you to come to Spain with us too! Bastian and Milo will be doing coupley things for their honeymoon, and I'll need my big strong bodyguard with me in case Dante is tied up in business." The sweet little man was laying it on thick, and judging by Sam's grin, he was eating it up with a spoon. "Besides, I want my bestie with me. Pleeease?" Ben's big eyes rounded even more and his lip popped out.

"Damn, I never should have taught you the puppy face," Sam smirked. "Okay, I'll go." Ben cheered, but Dante only rolled his eyes.

"Yes, a free trip halfway across the world is *such* a hardship."

"Hey, I'm here for my bestie," Sam shrugged. "Okay babe, let's go get changed for the party."

"*I* will take him to get changed," Dante growled.

"Fine, but keep it in your pants, old man. The party won't wait for you to try and get it up." Sam zipped out of the room just as Dante was reaching for his throat.

"That man makes my blood boil," Dante muttered.

"I'm sorry, osito," Ben said, his lip still poking out. "Take me upstairs and I'll make you feel all better." In a blink, Dante scooped up his giggling husband and disappeared.

"What about you, Milo?" Bastian asked, combing his fingers through my hair. "Would you like to change into something more comfortable?"

"I think I'd like to stay in this," I replied, smoothing my hand over the soft fabric of my trench coat. "I really do love it."

Bastian hummed and pecked my lips. "It makes me so happy to shower you with gifts." I had no doubt; since he rescued me from Jerome's house, Bastian had bought me something every single day, from clothes to fancy soaps to jewelry and everything in between.

"I love everything you buy for me, Papi, but you know I don't expect anything from you, right? Just being together is all the gift I'll ever need."

"My love, that only makes me want to spoil you more." I chuckled and Bastian took my lips in a hungry kiss. We were interrupted by the sound of people entering the room. The coven was pouring into the room in droves, all of them stopping by to give their congratulations and welcome me into the group. My heart had never been so full.

"You ready to party?" Sam asked when he, Ben and Dante arrived. I smiled at my friends; Sam was dressed in tight jeans and a sheer cropped top, looking like he could parade into any gay club in town and have his pick of the men. Ben had on his signature long cardigan and a nice pair of khakis. Dante was in designer jeans, a dress shirt and a blazer. And then there was Bastian and me in our trench coats with blood vials around our necks. We couldn't be more different, but that's what made us all so great together.

"Hell yeah," I answered, and my friends cheered.

"*I hope you like the party I've arranged for you,*" Bastian told me mentally with a concerned expression.

"*Papi, you know what I like. I'm sure this will be the best party any of us has ever seen.*" He smiled and lifted my knuckles to his lips for a gentle kiss.

Good lord, I was right about the party. Bastian went all out; he hired a heavy metal band to perform live as fog machines pumped clouds across the floor and lasers swirled in every direction. Bodies jumped and crashed together in excitement. The energy in the room was palpable, creating an electric tingle that danced across my skin.

It was a little comical watching Dante try to dance to the music. I was sure the guy had some serious moves when it came to ballroom dancing or ballet, given his natural grace and balance, but he was just not digging the pounding drums and screeching guitars. He kept stumbling and getting flustered when he ran into the person next to him. So, he instead busied himself by making sure everyone kept a respectable distance from his husband, who was happily bobbing along to the beat.

Sam, however, had no trouble. He was sandwiched between two guys as they bounced and gyrated, and I was sure their time together wouldn't end here, though whether they'd make it up to Sam's place or just end up in the restroom was unclear. Everyone else seemed to be having a great time, smiling and headbanging and screaming along to the lyrics. It felt amazing to have people who shared my interests.

And then there was Bastian. My wonderful man who put all of this together looked right in his element. He was moshing, thrashing and jumping like a pro. I was sure he didn't have much experience in this sort of thing, but he was trying his damndest to do what made me happy. He succeeded ten fold.

"*Thank you for this.*" It was too noisy in here for Bastian to hear my words, except for in his mind.

He stopped bouncing and gave me a huge grin. "*Anything for you, my love.*"

"*I've got an idea how to thank you properly,*" I offered, biting my lip.

"*Cielito, you don't have to thank me for...wait, what are you thinking?*" he asked when he caught my naughty suggestion.

"I'm thinking maybe we could slip away for a...private celebration."

Bastian's eyes darkened and he licked a slow line across his lips, making my knees weak. Before we could move, however, a cry of, *'This is amazing!'* caught our attention. I looked toward the sound and laughed out loud when I saw Ben crowd-surfing over the masses.

"Be careful, Amorcito!" Dante yelled as he pushed his way through the crowd after his husband. "And if any of you drop my sweet Benny, you shall lose your heads!" I quickly looked to Sam to get his attention, but saw he was already watching with a huge grin and recording the whole thing on his phone.

I laughed again and told Bastian as I watched Ben get passed around, *"Okay, I think it's safe to leave now. I'm pretty sure that was the highlight of the party."* I turned my head to look at my lover and was taken aback by the heat and intensity in his eyes.

He palmed my cheek and slowly trailed his thumb over my bottom lip as his eyes tracked the movement. *"The highlight of the party, perhaps, but sweet Milo, I promise you the best part of the night is yet to come."*

Chapter Thirteen

Bastian

I scooped my mate into my arms. I could smell his arousal that bloomed after my promise, and feel his need and lust in the air. As I carried him to the edge of the dance floor, the crowd parted to let us through. All of the vampires we passed wore knowing grins, but said nothing. Except Sam; he shouted lewd suggestions and I planned to do them all. Ben merely waved after he was safe on the ground again and told us to have fun. Dante was too busy checking his husband for nonexistent injuries to notice us leaving.

Not patient enough for the elevator, I dashed up the stairs with my beloved cradled against my chest. When I stopped in front of our apartment door, I noticed Milo's eyes were wide and his arms were tight around my neck.

"Are you okay, Cielito?"

"Yeah," he answered, blinking rapidly and appearing to come back to himself. "I've just never gone that fast before. Especially up stairs."

"Forgive me, Milo; I forgot you are not used to moving at such speed. I will be more mindful in the future."

"Trust me, I'm not complaining," he smirked. "I was just as excited to get home as you were." Hearing him refer to our apartment as 'home' still gave me goosebumps. I kissed him soundly before unlocking the door and carrying him inside.

"Where to, my love?" Lately, Milo and I had been on a mission of making love in every room and every surface of the apartment, claiming it and marking it as our own. It was Milo's idea and I didn't fight him on it for obvious reasons.

Milo ran his fingers through my long curls and gifted me with a beautiful smile. "I want you to take me to bed."

It was a bit tame considering the last time we were together, Milo fucked me as I was bent over the coffee table (which was on wheels, so we scooted all around the floor, successfully branding the entire living room), but whatever made him happy. I'd give myself to him anywhere, anytime he chose. "Your wish is my command." I walked halfway to our room, but stopped when I noticed Milo chewing on his lip.

"I'm not sure you understand, Papi," he said quietly, looking deep into my eyes. "I want *you* to take me to bed."

Oh. Ohhhh. My cock thickened in my trousers at the thought of topping sweet Milo for the first time. "Are you sure?" I felt no uncertainty or trepidation coming from him, but I wanted to hear it from his own lips.

"Yes," he answered confidently. "Bastian, I want everything with you. My body has had time to heal, and your love has healed my heart and soul. I know you would never hurt me, and you're the first man I've ever *wanted* to share this with. I'm not scared or nervous or unsure. I want this if you want it too."

"Oh Milo," I whispered, resting my forehead on his, "Thank you for your beautiful words. And thank you for your trust and faith in me." I kissed his lips and gazed into his beautiful dusky eyes. "I want everything with you too."

Milo smirked. "Then what are we waiting-" before he could finish his sentence, we were in the bedroom. He tipped his head back and laughed as I set him on his own two feet. He stopped laughing, however, when I sank my fingers into his shaggy hair and pulled his lips to mine.

The kiss started out sweet as we pecked and nibbled each other's lips, but soon turned heated. Milo opened readily when I ran my tongue along the seam of his lips. Our slick tongues glided across each other and we swallowed down one another's moans and whimpers.

Milo quickly but carefully unbuttoned my coat as I ravaged his lips. He pulled away and unbuttoned his as well. I shrugged my cloak off my shoulders and he collected both before hanging them on knobs on the dresser. It made me smile how cautious he was with the fabric; I was pleased to have picked something for him that he enjoyed.

When Milo returned to me, he was no longer gentle. He gripped the back of my head and pulled me down to him, taking my lips in a fiery kiss. He plunged his tongue into my mouth and licked every surface of my tongue and cheeks. He clawed at my shirt, popping two buttons off of the fabric in his haste. My lover was frantic to get to my body and it was the sexiest thing I'd ever experienced.

After Milo pushed my top off of my shoulders and onto the floor, I gripped each side of his collar and pulled, ripping the fabric to shreds, which floated to the floor. "Fuck, I love how strong you are," Milo panted. His eyes were wild with need. He lurched forward and licked a hot line over my mating scar, making my skin tingle and my body shiver. I curled my fingers over the top of his jeans, but he grabbed my hands. "Wait, wait, wait, I like these pants!"

I chuckled as Milo unfastened his own jeans and removed his boots. I did the same, and soon we were both naked and feasting on each other with our eyes. Both of our cocks were tall, hard and leaking. Milo was the first to draw his gaze away as he turned and climbed onto the bed. He stopped on the edge, supported on his hands and knees. He was completely spread and exposed to me; every inch of his cock, balls and pucker were on display for me, making my mouth water.

Milo looked over his shoulder at me. "Take me, Papi." He wrapped his fingers around his dick and gave himself a slow pull. "Please Bastian, I need you." I managed to tear my eyes away from the heart-stopping sight to grab our giant lube bottle from the nightstand, tossing it on the mattress by Milo's knee.

And then I dove in. I palmed his cheeks and spread them apart, flexing his hole. I leaned in and pressed my tongue to his wrinkled flesh, moaning as his musky-sweet flavor, which was intense after our evening of celebrating, burst across my tongue. Nothing in this world was as delicious as Milo's pucker. Unless it was

Milo's blood. Or Milo's lips. Every part of my lover was delectable.

I flicked my tongue across his opening as Milo pushed back, desperate for my touch. I wriggled the tip inside him, lapping at his walls and suckling against his rim. Milo gripped the sheets and rocked his hips back, forcing me further inside him. I devoured my mate's perfect asshole until he was whimpering and pleading for my cock.

I pumped a generous glob of lube onto my palm and spread it over my fingers. I wanted to make sure and have enough to make our lovemaking pleasurable for Milo. I knew I was quite large and would need to stretch and prepare him; I wouldn't hurt my mate for the world.

I pressed a slick fingertip to Milo's hole and massaged around his thick rim. He moaned at my touch, but didn't press back like he did for my tongue. He wanted me to take my time and get his body fully ready for me. When his ring of muscle thinned under my touch, I slipped just my fingertip inside him.

"Is this okay?" I asked quietly. I kept my voice and body language soft to keep Milo relaxed, and to let him know I was listening.

"Yes," he answered just as quietly. "You take such good care of me, Bastian."

"Always," I promised. I slid my hand forward slowly until my finger was fully inside him. After a moment of letting him get used to the size, I pumped it back and forth.

"Oh Papi," Milo moaned, tipping his head back until it met his shoulders. "That feels incredible."

I pumped even more lube onto my hand, not caring when it dripped down and collected on the blanket. I slowly added a second finger inside him, and only got whimpers and sweet moans in return. I pulsed my digits in and out of him, twisting and separating them to stretch Milo's tight channel. His inner walls hugged my fingers snugly; he wasn't ready for me yet. When I slid in a third finger, Milo hissed at the intrusion.

"Too much?"

"No," he answered, shaking his head. "It burns, but it's good."

I knew the pleasant burn he spoke of; I experienced it every time my lover entered me. I held my fingers still so that Milo could acclimate to them, but his channel pulsed around my digits, slowly sucking them further inside. When I could go no further, I pulled them back and pushed forward again. This time, I didn't hear a hiss, only a throaty moan.

I stretched and worked open Milo's tight little hole. When I added a fourth finger, he didn't even notice. My digits moved freely about and had more room to twist and scissor as he spread for me. When my lover was once again begging for me to fuck him, I removed my fingers.

I slathered my cock in lube and pressed my tip to Milo's readied entrance. "Take a deep breath, Cielito. I'm going to go slow, and I need for you to tell me if it gets to be too much, okay?" My lover nodded his understanding and took a deep breath. I pressed forward until my mushroom tip breached his entrance. When I was met with resistance, I massaged Milo's lower back to relax him and he pushed down against me, allowing me to pop through his inner muscles.

His body gripped and sucked me, begging me to bury myself in his tight heat, but I willed myself to go slowly. I entered him an inch at a time, then waited for him to get used to my size before I pushed in a little more. Finally, I was fully immersed in his heavenly body. My brow was covered in sweat from holding back.

Milo looked back at me and my spirit sank at the sight of his watery eyes and trembling lip. I thought for sure he was experiencing discomfort, and I was ready to pull free from him and offer myself to him instead, when his words stopped me.

"It doesn't hurt, Papi," he said in a warbled voice. A tear slipped down his cheek as he repeated, "It doesn't hurt."

My heart broke and soared at once. I hated that my beloved endured any pain in his past, but was jubilant I could provide him with a positive experience.

"I'm so glad, Cielito," I whispered. "I only want to make you feel pleasure." He gave me a pretty smile before turning to face forward once more. I inched my cock back until just my crown remained inside him, and slowly pushed back in as Milo keened long and loud.

Again and again I slowly pistoned my hips, nearly slipping free of my lover before sliding fully inside. Soon, I was gliding easily back and forth, and Milo begged me to go faster. Wanting to give him everything he needed, I picked up the pace, snapping my hips back and forth. I moaned at the sight of his ass gobbling up every inch of my cock.

I gripped Milo's hips and pushed him back onto me as I rocked inside him. My lover laid his chest flat on the bed and reached back for me. I knew what he wanted. I released his hips and gripped his hands, using them as leverage to grind back and forth. Milo and I always held hands when we made love. Even if our bodies were thrashing together, we still linked our fingers in a tender gesture.

Milo's hands squeezed mine as he cried out. "Oh god, Papi, you're grinding against my prostate! Please, more! Right there!"

I planted my feet on the floor and gripped his hands tighter before slamming inside him. I pulsed my hips back and forth, only pulling out about an inch each time, giving all of my attention and friction to Milo's sweet spot.

"Oh fuck...oh yes..." Milo turned his head to the side against the blanket, and I could see his eyes were squinted shut and his breaths were coming quickly through puffed cheeks. I quickened my pace even more, fucking in and out of him at a frantic tempo. "Oh god, Bastian, I'm getting close!"

I folded his hands over his lower back and pushed down, trapping his cock between his stomach and the mattress so he could get friction over his sensitive flesh. I crashed our hips together, hurtling his body forward and back, rubbing his cock into the blankets. Milo screamed and chanted my name as he writhed against the covers, humping back into me.

"Bastian! *Papi*!" I felt the moment my beloved reached climax, as his asshole clenched and pulsed around me. Milo's body trembled, sending shockwaves down my heated flesh and into my sack, which rolled and lifted toward my pelvis.

I screamed my lover's name as I buried myself in his tight channel and erupted. I pumped him full of my seed for the first time, marking him on the inside as I had the outside. He was mine. And I was his.

It took several minutes for us to catch our breath. I released Milo's hands to gently spread apart his cheeks and slowly pull my softening cock from his body. I pressed the pad of my thumb to his well-loved hole and massaged his swollen flesh. Some of my cum dripped from him, and I smoothed it over his skin.

"That feels good," Milo moaned. His voice was thick with satisfaction and sleepiness. "Everything you do to me just feels so damn good."

I leaned down and kissed a line up his spine, stopping to peck each bump of bone. When I reached his neck, I nipped at his mating scar, causing his body to quake. I chuckled and lowered my mouth to his ear. "Would you like to take a hot shower with me? I'll scrub your beautiful body and massage your muscles under the jets."

"That sounds amazing, but..." he looked back at me, worrying his bottom lip. "Can we just stay like this for a little while?" I smiled from ear to ear; my beloved was savoring the feel of my seed inside him as much as I was enjoying the knowledge it was there.

"Of course, Cielito. Come, let me get you covered up so that you are warm." I lifted him up and pulled down the corner of the blankets before settling him onto the mattress, his head cradled on his pillow. I wasn't concerned with the mess on top of the covers; I'd change them once Milo was resting peacefully, as I didn't need as much sleep as him.

"I love when you worry about me," he said, cuddling up to my side once I was lying beside him.

"I shall always worry about you, and do everything in my power to make you comfortable."

"I know you will." Milo snuggled up closer to me. "That was amazing, Bastian. I never thought it could be that wonderful. I mean, I never doubted it would be great with you or that you'd take care of me, I just..." he sighed. "I'm sorry, I don't know what I'm trying to say."

"I understand," I told him as I combed my fingers through his hair.

"I guess that's the best part of having a soulmate, right? That we understand each other so well?"

"One of the many, many best parts," I smiled.

"I just can't get over how lucky I am that you found me that night. If you hadn't been in town, or if you'd gotten tied up at the bookstore, it may have been too late."

A growl of anguish sounded in my chest, and Milo was quick to rub it away. "I'm sorry, Cielito, but I cannot bear to think of such things."

"Then let's not," he replied, wrapping his arm around my waist. "I'm here and you're here, and we're together forever, right?"

"Forever."

Milo was silent for several moments, and I wondered if he'd fallen asleep when he said, "Hey Papi?"

"Yes, my love?"

"I decided what I want to do with the money you gave me when we met. Remember when you said you wanted me to spend it on something that makes me happy?"

"Of course." I turned my head and peeked down at him, excited to hear what he'd come up with.

"I want to get a matching wing tattooed on the left side of my chest, to symbolize the angel that saved me."

My heart nearly burst from my chest at his gratitude and thoughtfulness. "Oh Milo," I whispered, pulling him as close to me as humanly possible, "You honor me."

"You honor me too," he said, drawing senseless patterns on my stomach with his fingertip. "I love you so much, Bastian." He kissed my chest. "For the rest of forever."

"I love you too, Milo. For all of eternity."

Milo hummed happily and let his hand stop and rest against my skin. "I think I'm going to take a little nap. Will you wake me up in like an hour for that amazing shower you mentioned?"

I chuckled and kissed the top of his head. "I promise, Cielito."

Within moments, my sleepy Milo was resting soundly. His breaths were deep and even against my side, and his heartbeat thumped steadily against my skin. No matter what he said, I knew *I* was the lucky one to have found him in that alleyway those few weeks ago. I didn't just find a lover; I found my alma gemela - my soulmate, my forever, my always. I found my strength, purpose, patience and love unmeasured.

I sighed happily and kissed Milo's wild, shaggy hair that I adored once more. And then I looked at the clock, watching for sixty minutes to pass so I could speak with my little heaven again.

The End

Thank you for reading *Twice Shy*! I hope you enjoyed the book! Stay tuned for Sam's story in the next and final book of the Javier Coven series, *Twice Bitten,* available now! *Look below for more titles by Jayda Marx.*

M/M Paranormal Romance:

Once Bitten: Javier Coven Book 1 (Vampire M/M)

Twice Shy: Javier Coven Book 2 (Vampire M/M)

Twice Bitten: Javier Coven Book 3 (Vampire M/M/M)

Untitled: Duff Coven Book 1 (Vampire M/M) Coming soon!

Mine to Save: Pine Ridge Pack Book 1 (M/M Wolf Shifter)

Mine to Keep: Pine Ridge Pack Book 2 (M/M Wolf Shifter)

Mine to Protect: Pine Ridge Pack Book 3 (M/M Wolf Shifter) Coming soon!

Shadow Walker: Bay City Coven Book 1 (Vampire M/M)

Into the Shadows: Bay City Coven Book 2 (Vampire M/M) Coming soon!

M/M Series:

Arrested Hearts Book 1: Gage & Tyson (M/M) *Can be read as standalone

Arrested Hearts Book 2: Chris & Lyle (M/M)

Arrested Hearts Book 3: Mike & Jonah (M/M)

Arrested Hearts Book 4: Sam & Jordan (M/M) Coming soon!

My Everything (M/M) *Can be read as standalone

My Forever (novella sequel to "My Everything") (M/M)

Head Over Wheels (M/M) *Can be read as standalone

Head Over Wheels: Book 2 (M/M)

Care for You (Head Over Wheels: Book 3) (M/M)

My Grumpy Old Bear (Loveable Grumps: Book 1) *Can be read as standalone

My Confused Cub (Lovable Grumps: Book 2) Coming soon!

Beautiful Dreamer (M/M Age Play) (Secret Desires: Book 1) *Can be read as standalone

Lost Boy (M/M BDSM) (Secret Desires: Book 2) Coming soon!

M/M Standalone

Ours to Love (M/M/M)

Chasing Jackson (M/M)

Nervous Nate (M/M Age Play Romance)

Valentine Shmalentine (M/M)

M/F Series:

Housewife Chronicles: Complete Series (M/F)

Luscious: Complete Series (M/F)

Manufactured by Amazon.ca
Bolton, ON